"We Need To Go Someplace Where The Kids Won't Find Us For A Few Minutes."

The sun was setting fast, and Craig's expression was shadowed in the blurry light. "I don't want them thinking up any more matchmaking schemes. Not just for our sakes, Karen. For theirs."

"I completely agree. They were hurt enough when we split up."

It never crossed her mind that he was reaching for her, until his hands were on her shoulders.

She'd thought the kids were the only things on his mind. She'd thought he'd written off their lovemaking on Saturday as the insane, mistaken, irresponsible encounter that it was.

"Dammit, Karen." His voice was the drug of a caress, whiskey-hoarse and low. "Be good," he scolded. But he was the one being wicked.

Dear Reader,

Joan Hohl is back! And I know you're all cheering at her return. Her *Man of the Month* book, *Convenient Husband,* is Joan at her steamiest, and her hero, Jasper (also known as "Main") Chance, is a man to remember. That's *all* I'm going to tell you about this sexy, sensuous story.... You'll just have to read it for yourself.

A book by Lass Small is always a treat, and you'll all be thrilled to know that *A Restless Man* is the first in her three-book series about those Fabulous Brown Brothers. (Yes, you first met Bob Brown in her 1991 *Man of the Month* book, *'Twas the Night.*) Look for more of the Brown men in October and December.

August is completed with a terrific story from Mary Lynn Baxter, *And Baby Makes Perfect* (another hero to remember!); *Just Like Old Times* by Jennifer Greene (watch out for the matchmaking teenagers!); *Midsummer Madness* by Christine Rimmer (with Cody McIntyre, town hunk); and *Sarah and the Stranger* by Shawna Delacorte, a new author you'll hear more of.

Next month, look for Silhouette Desire books by some of your favorite authors, including Annette Broadrick, Diana Palmer and Helen R. Myers.

All the best,

Lucia Macro
Senior Editor

JENNIFER GREENE
JUST LIKE OLD TIMES

SILHOUETTE *Desire*®

Published by Silhouette Books New York

America's Publisher of Contemporary Romance

SILHOUETTE BOOKS
300 East 42nd St., New York, N.Y. 10017

JUST LIKE OLD TIMES

ISBN: 0-373-05728-8

First Silhouette Books printing August 1992

Printed in the U.S.A.

JENNIFER GREENE

lives near Lake Michigan with her husband and two children. Before writing full-time, she worked as a personnel manager, teacher and college counselor. Michigan State University honored her as an "outstanding woman graduate" for her work with women on campus.

Ms. Greene has written over thirty-five category romances for which she has won many awards, including the RITA for Best Short Contemporary book from Romance Writers of America and "Best Series Author" from *Romantic Times*. She previously wrote under the pen name of Jeanne Grant.

One

"**D**ad? I'm worried about Mom."

Craig Reardon bent over the lawn-mower motor and pulled out the dipstick. "We've been through this before, Julie. What your mother does is no longer any of my business."

"But she's been dating this guy—"

"Which is even less of my business. Or yours, or your brother's. Your mother is entitled to a private life." The sucker needed oil again, Craig thought. Was anything going to go right today?

His daughter trailed him into the toolshed. "But this guy talked her into going up to the cabin this weekend."

"Sweetheart, how many times do we have to talk about this? Your mother has the right to date every man in Colorado Springs if she's so inclined. That's part of what being divorced means." He twisted a nozzle onto the new can of oil and stalked back into the blinding sunshine. It had to be a hundred and ten in the sun. He wanted to mow the lawn like he wanted to chew nails. And Julie was still hounding his footsteps.

"But she *hasn't* dated before this, Dad. Nobody. And this guy has been moving in on her real hard—"

"Your mother can handle herself. Believe me. In a ring with a pit bull and your mother, she'd come out ahead."

"Not with this guy. I'm telling you he's real bad news. He's about a million pounds bigger than she is, and I don't trust him and I don't like him and he scares me."

"Scares you? He did something to scare you?" Craig's head jerked up from the lawn mower, the oil forgotten. His gaze lasered on his daughter's face. "Has this jerk laid a hand on you? Said anything to you?"

"Not to me. To *Mom*. He lies to her and she doesn't see it. I don't think she should go up to the cabin with him. There's no one around there. And you know Mom's naive—"

"Your mother doesn't have a naive bone in her entire body."

Julie said, "I think he's gonna do something to her."

"Sweetheart, no one is going to do anything to your mother that she doesn't want—not in this life. She'd level anyone who tried."

"Did she ever level you, Dad?"

"Yes." Craig glowered at his youngest. "And that's enough on this whole subject. I've told you and told you—I'll talk about anything you want, anytime you want. Except for your mother. Clear?"

"Mom? It's your turn to use the cabin this weekend, right?"

"Right. Only I doubt that we'll make it up there, Jon. There's just too many chores to do around home." Karen flopped the sack of groceries on the table, set down her briefcase and untwisted the purse from her shoulder. What a day. She'd bought something for dinner, but darned if she could remember what it was.

"Good thing."

"Hmm? What's a good thing?" Chops. Grilled on the barbecue. That's what she'd planned for dinner— assuming she could get the dratted barbecue to work. The last time she tangled with the relic, she'd singed her bangs and nearly set fire to the porch.

"It's a good thing you aren't up there, because I think Dad forgot it was your weekend. He's already planning on using the cabin."

"Oh? Well, that's okay." She turned toward the freezer with two bags of frozen vegetables in her hands, only to find her son's sixteen-year-old gangly frame blocking the way. There was guilt in his eyes and a half gallon of milk en route to his mouth. "*Not* from the carton, Jon Jacob. You know better. Is Julie still at your father's?"

"Yeah. Said she'd be back by seven. He's taking someone up there, Mom. To the cabin. This weekend."

"That's nice."

"A woman."

"That's nice," Karen repeated vaguely. Again she turned, this time toward the cupboard by the sink. Defying both logic and gravity, her son managed to be directly in her path—again.

"You don't care?"

"Come on, Jon. We've been over this a hundred times. Your father is a free man. He's entitled to companionship, and what he does with his private time is his business. Not yours or Julie's. And definitely not mine. Not anymore."

"But what if he was in trouble?"

"Your father was made for trouble. He *loves* trouble. Believe me, he can take care of himself. Now let's just call this subject off-limits and drop it."

"Her name is Diedre."

"Jon—"

"She's a real piece of work. Long legs, hair down her back, a body like you can't believe—"

"Jonathan Jacob—"

"And young."

Young. The word stung like a wasp bite, making Karen rub two fingers on her temples. She didn't have a headache, but she was getting one. "I don't want to hear any more," she said firmly. *Where* were the darned potatoes? She couldn't possibly have gone to the grocery store and forgotten potatoes. Again.

"She acts real nice, but she isn't nice, Mom. She wears this strong perfume that could make you gag. And her fingernails are like claws." Her son lifted his hands, illustrating a classic pose for Dracula. "She took one look at Dad and you could practically see the dollar signs light up in her eyes. She's been chasing after him like you wouldn't believe. Dad just doesn't see what's going on. And do you know what she told Julie?"

"No, and I don't care what she told your sister. This conversation is over. And this time, I mean it." Finally she found the sack of potatoes.

"She told Julie that she was coming back from the cabin this weekend with a ring."

"A ring?"

"She said Dad was going to ask her to marry him."

Karen didn't mean to plop the sack on the counter so hard. It just . . . happened. Making a fitting finale for a perfectly terrible day, the plastic bag split open. Twenty pounds of potatoes spilled helter-skelter down the counter, in the sink, on the floor.

With every hairpin turn, Karen left civilization farther behind. It was cooler in the mountains, quieter. Towns disappeared, roads dropped away. Spruce and fir climbed the steep rocky slopes, thick green nests of them that fringed the mountain peaks. Higher yet, the air was so sharp and rare that it stung her lungs. She caught a glimpse of water below—just a glint of fast-moving diamonds in the sun—and knew she was close.

A deer shot across the road as she made the last turn. After that, only a dirt track twisted up for another quarter mile. If she took her eyes off the path for even seconds, she risked barreling down the steep ravine.

To heck with the ravine—she checked her appearance in the rearview mirror. Yesterday she'd packed a haircut into an already busy schedule. She'd also raided the local drugstore for all-new cosmetics.

No one could tell that she'd fussed. She looked exactly as she was supposed to look—a woman dressed for a camping weekend. Her shirt was coral, her best color, and her khaki jeans were slimming and snug, but the clothes were recognizably practical. The sweep of blush on her cheeks could be taken for natural color. Her lip gloss was excusable as a sunscreen. A sparing brush of mascara had darkened the pale tips of her eyelashes, and another woman had no way of knowing that her hair rarely looked this good.

You look terrific, she mentally assured herself. Yet the puckish frown on her brow refused to disappear. No pep talk on self-confidence was going to make her younger than thirty-six, add inches to her five-foot-five-inch frame or add any sultry glamour to her looks.

Since Thursday night, the name "Diedre" had gnawed on her mind like a toothache. Her imagination had easily embellished her son's description of the woman. Anyone named Diedre had to be tall and svelte and sexually sophisticated, and Craig wouldn't waste time on a bimbo. The woman had to be smart. She was probably a creative wonder in bed. She had long hair. She was young.

Karen chewed her bottom lip as the cabin came in sight. A dusty white Jeep Cherokee was already parked on the knoll, so Craig was here. He'd probably driven up last night. With *her*.

She braked behind the Cherokee and turned the key. Nerves bounced in her stomach like restless gnats. It was her scheduled weekend at the cabin; she had absolutely every right to be here. The kids were stashed at her dad's house. She'd stolen a few hours alone at the cabin many times before. Craig had no reason to suspect there was anything strange about her being here, and at the last minute she'd even thought to bring a "prop." The travel bag was stuffed with apples, bulging and heavy enough to look like a day's change of clothes. Karen didn't need clothes. She didn't plan to stay more than ten minutes. Long enough to establish her alibi—that it was Craig who'd mixed up the weekends, not her—and to catch a look at his *Diedre*.

Karen grabbed the tote and climbed out of the car, feeling judicious and righteous. Any good mother made sacrifices for her children. Personally Karen couldn't care less about the woman. The divorce had been final for a year. If Craig wanted to take up with a selfish, avaricious sexual Amazon, it was his problem. But if the woman was a potential stepmother—if the relationship was serious—she would obviously have an effect on the children's lives.

Karen just wanted to look at the turkey.

For the kids' sake.

No mother would do less.

She sucked in her stomach, straightened her spine and fixed a secure, serene, mature smile on her face. If they were still in bed, she was going to die. It was almost eleven o'clock. She'd made very sure of not arriving any earlier. Surely eleven was amply late in the morning for both of them to long be up?

A raven flew overhead. She thought glumly of omens. Sun speckled through the tree branches, silvering the rock-strewn path. The cabin sat on a knoll, overlooking a vista of jutting cliffs and a distant valley. In a few weeks the quaking aspens in the yard would turn gold. Now, in early September, their leaves shivered for the barest puff of wind.

Karen felt a kissing-cousin kinship with the quaking aspen. Her heart was thudding like a trapped cat's, her palms wet with nerves. Her gaze swept over the rough-stone cabin.

It was the only bond left from their marriage. The cabin was still in both their names. Their respective divorce lawyers, months back, had explained what an impossible and terrible legal idea that was. She and Craig had paid no attention. The kids loved the cabin. Neither parent wanted to be deprived of the right to take them up here. They'd worked out scheduled times on a calendar, so neither intruded on the other, and both did caretaking chores. Craig had seen to the new roof, always left a stack of wood. She did minor carpentry, made sure the place was stocked with emergency canned goods. The arrangement worked. Maybe when the kids were grown, they'd have to make other choices—but the kids weren't grown yet.

Thinking of the children again strengthened her resolve. She wasn't sure what all the nerves were about, anyway. She'd be gone ten minutes from now. Anybody could live through anything for ten minutes.

She crossed the wide stone porch. The front door was ajar, but the inner screen door was aggravatingly too dense to see through. She hesitated, unsure how to behave naturally in the situation when there was nothing natural, ethical or right about spying on her ex-husband.

She reminded herself—again—that she wasn't here for Craig, but for the children.

Briskly she rapped on the doorframe, once, loudly, and then poked her head inside. "Craig?" Her voice sounded tinny, like a laryngitic frog. A guilty frog. "Craig?" she called again.

"Karen?"

She thought that he must have a sore throat because something was wrong with his voice, too. Her ex-husband normally had a rich, throaty tenor. She'd never heard his voice rasp in that strangely artificial baritone.

It took a minute for her eyes to adjust after being in bright sunlight, but quickly, too quickly, she realized that Craig was fresh out of bed. When he turned at the sound of her voice, he was standing at the wood stove with a spatula in his hand. His dark blond head was tousled, his bronze chest bare and he was wearing nothing but old jeans.

Her gaze whipped away from his bare chest. He started talking at the same instant she did, but Karen barely heard him. Words tripped out of her mouth faster than a babbling brook.

"Heavens, I'm so embarrassed! I saw your car out there, but until then I had no idea—none!—that you were here. I thought it was my weekend.... I could have sworn it was my weekend...." There were two bedrooms overlooking the cliffside. Both doors were open. She could see a navy blue sleeping bag, but the bag was lying flat with no telltale bulge of a voluptuous female body inside it.

She put her hand on her heart. "I could shoot myself. Just plain shoot myself." The bathroom door was also ajar. No movement there, and there was no other place for a body to hide. The main room was huge and open, combining the living area and kitchen, the stone fireplace at one end and the wood stove at the other. Between the stripped oak walls were an oversize couch and easy chairs, Indian rugs and pottery and an antique gaming table where they used to play chess and cards. She saw a man's shirt, but no sign of anything feminine or female. In the kitchen corner, copper pots and pans hung from the ceiling, and behind the round oak table there were cupboards. Small cupboards. The closet door was closed, but Karen knew it was too stuffed with sporting goods and spare coats for a body to squeeze in there.

Craig smacked his forehead with an open palm. "Damn! It *is* your weekend, isn't it? I must have gotten the date confused. It was a bitch of a week at work, and I guess I just didn't look at the calendar. I apologize—"

"It's all right. Don't worry about it. In fact, I'll be glad to leave. I shouldn't have come up here as it was. I really only had a few hours free and the kids were with my dad and—"

"Karen, what on earth is wrong with your neck?"

"My neck?" Her palm swept up to her throat, but Craig was no longer looking at her. His gaze darted behind her, first left, then right, then narrowly out the screen door. There was nothing wrong with *her* neck. It was his that was craned around like an ostrich's. "Are you looking for something?"

Immediately he straightened. "Looking for someone? Why on earth would I be looking for someone?"

Confused, she pushed a hand through her hair. "I didn't ask if you were looking for someone. I asked if you were looking for some*thing*."

"Well, I wasn't. I was just making breakfast. I came up here last night after work, and... Karen, something *is* wrong with your neck. Did you pull a muscle?"

"Hmm?" Where *was* the blasted woman? The only boots in sight were a distinctly huge size twelve. The woman could have gone for a morning swim in the creek, but Craig would never have let her go alone. The current was too swift, the water cramp cold. Years ago, the one time Karen had stolen off for a swim alone, Craig had come pelting down the ravine to tear a strip off her hide. She could still remember...

"If you left something in the car, don't hesitate to go get it."

Her gaze swiveled back to his face again. She frowned in bewilderment. Something was wrong with him. Sore throat or no sore throat, her ex-husband had never talked to her in that strange hearty baritone. And his comment made no sense. She patted her bulging tote. "This was all I brought with me. I was only going to be here for a few hours. And even if I left something in the car, I wouldn't be bringing it up—I just told you I was leaving. It doesn't matter if you mixed up the weekends. Like I explained, I have a million things to do at home, so there's no reason you shouldn't be the one to stay.... Craig, what *are* you looking for?"

"Him." The word popped out of his mouth, unbidden, unexpected, sneaked out like a secret told that was supposed to be kept.

"Him who?" Craig had a million flaws, all of which she knew intimately, but being batty had never been one of them. "Who on earth are you talking about?"

"*Him*, Karen. Oh, hell." He stalked past her for the screened door and impatiently pushed it open.

She stepped closer and they both peered out. Her Cierra was neatly parked behind his Cherokee. The sun shone. A breeze rustled through the treetops. But there was absolutely no other sign of movement beyond a squirrel leaping through the yard.

"You didn't bring anyone with you?" Craig was still looking out. As far as Karen could tell, he was looking just about everywhere but at her.

"No, I didn't bring anyone with me. Why would I bring anyone with me? I told you the kids were at Dad's...." She hesitated, and then asked casually, "Did *you* happen to bring anyone with you?"

Craig swung the screen door closed. "No. I came alone. Is there some reason you'd think that I had someone with me?"

"Heavens, no. The thought never crossed my mind. I was just making conversation. After all, you *could* have brought someone and..."

Karen's voice petered out like a deflated balloon. She swallowed, suddenly aware how close Craig was. He shifted back as quickly as she did, but for the first time he looked straight in her eyes. Her pulse bucked uneasily. He wasn't smiling, but there was a shadow of humor in his shrewd brown eyes, and a glint of stark honesty. She hadn't shared anything as intimate as honesty with her ex-husband in a very long time.

"What the hell is going on here?" he murmured.

She took a breath. "I don't know."

"Do you have the feeling that something isn't ko-sher in Denmark?"

She nodded cautiously.

"Did you think I had a woman up here?"

Damn him. When push came down to shove, Craig had always been blunt as a brick. She said swiftly, "It was none of my business. I know that, and I'm sorry—honestly, miserably sorry—for barging in on your privacy. There's no excuse. I feel stupid and I feel awful. It was just that Jon told me—"

"Karen?" When he interrupted her, the fakey hoarse baritone was gone from his voice. "Julie told me you were bringing a man up here for the week-end."

An awkward silence fell between them. Karen finally broke it. "I don't understand—I have to no idea—why Julie would have told you that."

"She also told me that the man was trouble. That you were in over your head. That she was afraid of this guy."

She shook her head. It still didn't clear the cob-webs of confusion. "Craig, that's ridiculous. I'm not involved with anyone. I haven't even dated anyone since..." She took another clipped breath. "Any-way. Jon told *me* that Diedre was a real fast number. That she was a taker, a con artist. And obviously that's none of my business, but he didn't seem to like her and he was all upset and I started worrying—"

"Diedre?"

There was something in his tone. She started to nod, then stopped. "I take it Jon Jacob slightly exagger-ated your imminent engagement?"

"Our son invented it out of thin air. I don't know any Diedre. Never dated any Diedre. Never met a woman named Diedre in my entire life."

Karen vaguely remembered falling flat on her face, first grade, the school Christmas play. It wasn't any more embarrassing than this. "I'm not sure what the children expected to accomplish with this little trick," she said slowly, "but if you don't mind, I'm going straight home to kill them both."

"Poison," he suggested.

"I was thinking more along the lines of slow strangling."

"That's good. Real good." He said absently, "Had breakfast?"

"Pardon?"

"Have you had breakfast? I was just putting some food together, and you just made a two-hour drive. I assume you could use a break before climbing back in a car again. At least have a cup of coffee—"

He'd offered the invitation impulsively. She doubted he meant it. "Craig, I don't want to be in your way."

"You're not in my way. And I think it should be a mutual decision which reform school we send our offspring to."

Her lips started to twitch. If she was embarrassed by the situation, at least he was, too. It couldn't do any harm to stay for a few more minutes, particularly when an easy topic of conversation was assured. They always got along when the subject was the kids. Usually, though, their conversation was about the children's welfare.

Mutually plotting the demise and immurement of their well-loved progeny struck Karen as an impossibly humorous change of pace.

She had, after all, only come up here for the kids' sake.

Two

———

They had pancakes heaped with sweet wild blueberries. She had seven. He had five. She sat at the table with a leg tucked under her, her eyes as dark and soft as the blueberries, devouring his pancakes with pure, sensual relish. He'd forgotten. His ex-wife had always had a weakness for certain foods. Pancakes was one of them.

"I've talked with them about the divorce a hundred times," she said honestly.

"So have I. And I know they've had a hard time adjusting, but it never once occurred to me that they were harboring ideas of our getting back together."

"You think that's why they made up those stories? To get us up here at the same time?"

"Come on, Kara. What else could it be?"

Her eyes flew to his, then skittered back to her coffee. He hadn't meant to call her "Kara". The old pet nickname just slipped out.

Craig lurched to his feet to put the frying pan in the sink. The sudsy water was hot to scalding. He needed that jolt of reality. His mind definitely wasn't on the kids.

Coming up here to save his ex-wife from some Don Juan lothario had been a stupid idea. In itself, that was no surprise. These days he had a six-figure income, an executive job and all the trappings that came with success. But he'd always excelled at making classically stupid moves around Karen.

Technically he'd lost the right to worry about her when the final divorce papers were signed. And Craig hadn't... until their fifteen-year-old daughter had described the kind of jerk Karen was seeing.

Nobody—no woman on this earth—could be more vulnerable, more susceptible to the wrong kind of man than his ex-wife.

He ought to know.

Driving up through the mountains last night, memories had trailed him as relentlessly as his taillights. He remembered, too well, the first time he'd laid eyes on her. Junior year. The first day of school. History class. She'd walked in and sat next to Rick Willming—her boyfriend at the time—and Craig had fallen hard. She was the most beautiful girl he'd ever seen. Everything about her was golden—her hair like streaked honey, her skin with a sun-kissed glow, her voice as soft as a melted butterscotch.

But Kara wouldn't give him the time of day.

He got rid of Willming. Then joined up for debate because she was in debate. Then starting hanging out after school at Old Man Simpson's because Simpson sold gourmet jelly beans and Kara was a sucker for them.

She still wouldn't give him the time of day.

He'd been a football star. All the girls had been impressed, except Karen. It could be that he had a teeny reputation for being wild and fast, and he figured she was scared of him. So he'd changed his ways, took up acting as saintly as a Boy Scout—walking her home, carrying her books, calling her every night—and never by word or deed implying that he had a live hormone in his entire body.

After a month—the longest month in his life—she'd tentatively agreed to go out with him. Once. Only to a movie and only if they were home by ten. He'd taken her to a Walt Disney. What else could he risk? And at five to ten, at her parents' back door, he'd kissed her good-night, without question the most tepid, careful kiss he'd ever given a girl. Swear to *Pete,* it was an accident that his hand had brushed her breast.

She'd socked him. A small golden fist—straight in the eye....

"Craig? There's about one last mug of coffee in the pot. You want it?"

His head jerked around. Karen had cleared the dishes and was standing beside him, a towel in her hand. "No. Thanks. And you don't have to do that."

"What, didn't you notice I ate half the food? If you're willing to wash, I don't mind drying." She cocked her head. "What's the frown for? Still thinking about the kids?"

"Not really." He hesitated. "Actually, I was thinking about a spring day and a canoe ride a long time ago. A kid showing off for his date, figuring he'd be real cool and show her how well he could handle white water."

She snatched a white plate from the rack and suddenly wiped it bone dry, with her head bent and the sunlight playing on the slender curve of her shoulders. "If I remember right, we ended up pretty wet."

They hadn't ended up wet. They'd ended up soaked, the canoe long gone and the two of them stranded on some bank in the middle of nowhere. Another time he'd conned her into skipping class for a picnic. They'd been caught, suffered a week's detention outside the principal's office. And yet another time he'd scraped together the money to take her for a really nice dinner. Only his aging jalopy had had a flat tire, on a night that was pouring rain. She'd got grease on her favorite white dress. Worse yet, she'd caught hell for being late when he finally got her home.

Karen had never been in trouble, until she'd met Craig. The one night he'd been determined that everything would go perfectly was the first time they made love.

She'd quit socking him by then. She'd quit batting at his hands. She was still scared but not unwilling, as caught up in the magic between them as he was. Only it was midwinter, in snowstorm-freezing temperatures, and the back seat of his car had no space. He was trying so hard to be cool and do everything right, only he didn't know how to do anything right and he was so crazy for her he couldn't think. He'd hurt her.

God, he didn't mean to. And when she'd started crying, he almost died.

Karen stole the sponge from the soapy water and whisked it over the counter. "Nearly done. Won't take us long to finish up now." She smiled at him, quick, and then turned away.

Craig sensed that she felt increasingly uncomfortable with him. It was his fault. He should have been making small talk, not strolling down a mental memory lane. Yet he hadn't been alone with Karen since he could remember. Either they were with the kids or they weren't together.

He hadn't looked at her—really looked—in years. He knew the seventeen-year-old girl she used to be, but it struck him with painful honesty that the grown woman next to him was a total stranger. He didn't know her at all.

Her coral shirt and casual slacks clung alluringly to her slim figure. They were just camping clothes, yet she wore them with a sense of style and natural elegance. Her face was still a delicate oval, fine boned with classic features, yet her forehead had the pale brush of character lines. She moved with a woman's assurance, a confidence that the girl-Karen never had. He had no idea what made her laugh anymore. No idea if she was still a sucker for gourmet jelly beans. No idea if she was as wild and sweet in bed with another man.

He didn't know her, Craig repeated to himself. Yet she was even more beautiful than she used to be—still golden, from her streaky hair to her honeyed skin— and there was still a hint in her soft blue eyes of the vulnerable girl she once was. The girl who believed in him, who trusted him, who followed him no matter how much terrible trouble he'd gotten them into—because she loved him. Once upon a time, Karen had loved and wanted him beyond rhyme, reason or sense. God, were they in love.

The pain was old, sharp, familiar. *How had they lost it? How could two people possibly lose something that rare, that special, that strong?*

Karen tossed down the sponge. "All done!" she said brightly. "Breakfast was great, thank you very much, and I'd better be on my way. Don't worry about the kids, I'll talk to them when I get home—"

"So will I."

"Okay."

"Maybe we'd better check back and compare notes. I think this is one of those problems where we need to present a united parental front."

Karen nodded agreement, but she barreled toward the door as if a ghost were nipping at her heels. If the screen door had been locked, she'd probably have gone through it. It wasn't locked; all she had to do was slap it open. Her feet hit the porch at a racing jog and kept on going. She heard Craig behind her; apparently he intended to see her to the car. She wished he wouldn't.

Blood was hurtling down her pulse, her nerves snappy and restless. For a few minutes over breakfast, they'd been okay together. It was her fault that the mood had changed. She was the one who'd dropped the conversation, allowed the awkward silence to loom between them until it was bigger than an unbridgeable wall. At least for her.

It had hit her suddenly, like the shock of a slap, that she was wiping pots and pans with a total stranger. Craig wasn't the boy she fell in love with. He wasn't the man she'd married. This tall broad-shouldered man with the electric dark eyes—she didn't know him at all.

How many years had it been since she'd looked at Craig? *Really* looked at him? He'd always been overpoweringly tall, always lean and muscular. But now his strong square features had the life lines of experience and his dark blond hair had a few threads of gray in the sideburns. He moved with quiet power and an intimidatingly shrewd awareness of everything around him. The boy-Craig had an overactive libido and no control. The grown-Craig was a physical, sexual man who made her think of dynamite on tap, vital, virile and nobody's fool. She guessed that very few dared to challenge him in a boardroom. She guessed that hundreds of women would be thrilled to challenge him in a bedroom.

Her feet skimmed over the grass.

It was time to hit the road when she started imagining her ex-husband in bedrooms. Worse yet, to imagine herself between a pair of silky sheets with him. The sudden leap of sexual awareness confused and mortified her, but thankfully Craig couldn't possibly know how she felt. She had other reasons for wanting—*needing*—to get away from her ex-husband. Now. Quickly. At rocket speeds, if she could only fly.

If the grown man had become a compelling stranger, there was still a hint in his grin of the brash, cocky boy who had once led her into so much trouble. Back then, Craig had no judgment and no brains and never once looked before he dived in deep water—but she'd never doubted that he loved her. Beyond reason, beyond rhyme or sense. They'd been crazy and they'd been stupid, but *God* had they been in love.

It wasn't supposed to hurt anymore. She'd sworn, sworn, *sworn* she wasn't going to let it hurt anymore. The divorce had been a relief and a release—for him, for her. She didn't want back in a relationship that had been miserably hurtful. Neither could he. Yet the never-answered question suddenly ached in her heart like a fresh, raw wound. *How had they lost it? How? How could two people possibly lose magic that incredibly strong?*

"Whoa, Matilda."

She reached the car, winded and breathless.

"Hey. Did I miss noticing a fire?"

Get a grip, Karen. You're acting like a total fool. "No fire," she said cheerily. "I just remembered what a long drive it was. I need to get back—for the children." The chrome door handle was within reach, as close as an arm's length, as close as escape.

If Craig hadn't been blocking the way. Sun streamed on his bronze shoulders, on his brown bare throat. She didn't mean to meet his eyes, didn't want to, but it was like fighting the pull of a magnet. His gaze, sharp and perceptive, lanced on her pale face so thoroughly that a shiver chased up her spine.

"Did I say something to upset you?" he asked quietly.

"Heavens, no. I'm not upset. I just have to go—"

"I understand. But you were in such a hurry that you forgot your tote, Kara."

He didn't seem to notice that he'd forgotten himself and called her Kara again. She pretended she hadn't heard. "Good grief, where's my head today? Thanks—" She reached for the bag, but as he started to hand it over, his palm cupped the base. His forehead pinched in a curious frown.

"What on earth do you have in this?"

"Nothing."

"Something's rolling in there. Something round—" He squeezed the worn canvas in several places, then glanced at her again.

He wasn't going to let it go. One of Craig's worst character flaws always was, always would be, an insatiable streak of curiosity. Karen pushed a hand through her hair, thinking that she might as well die and go to hell and get it over with. "Apples," she said flatly.

"Apples? You have to be kidding." He unzipped the tote several inches and peered in. "Apples," he announced. His voice was deadpan, but she saw it—the ghost of an unholy grin lurking at the edges of his mouth, boyish and more wicked than sin.

She didn't want to make him smile—not at her, not again. It was that rash, dangerous grin that unraveled her senses a million years ago. How could it still have so much power? "There's a perfectly logical reason why I put apples in there," she said defensively.

"What? Come on, 'fess up. I can't stand it," he coaxed.

"If I'd packed clothes, they would have been all wrinkled. The weight and bulge of the apples—I thought they would make it look like a filled overnight bag." Hell and damnation, her cheeks burned hotter than fire. "Okay, okay, so you caught me—I fibbed. I already knew you were up here and I was never going to stay. Not if you were with...a woman."

An enigmatic light glinted in his eyes. He tossed the bag through the open window into the back seat, but his gaze never left her face. "I almost forgot about Daphne."

"Diedre," she corrected him. "And when I get a hold of *your* son, he's going to wish he never thought up the name."

Again his lips twitched. "Did *your* son ever happen to mention what this Diedre looked like?"

Karen rolled her eyes to the sky. "Luxurious dark hair as long as her behind. Legs that wouldn't quit. Long fingernails, sultry eyes, an Amazon in height. I had her pictured as a centerfold with claws—which, now that I think about it, should have tipped me off that our sixteen year old's hormonal imagination was working overtime. But he made her sound like she was sneaky and calculating, terribly selfish, and I..." She suddenly swallowed. "I need to get going."

"Kara—"

"I *really* need to get going," she said firmly.

"And you can. In a second. But I owe you a thank-you first."

"A thank-you?"

"You went to a lot of trouble, stuffing those apples in your bag, driving all the way up here. It sounds like Jon Jacob painted a picture of a real man-eating witch."

She shook her head. "He painted the picture of a beautiful woman, and I had absolutely no business interfering—"

"You were worried about me."

"No."

"You were worried about me," he repeated gently. "And I owe you a thank-you."

She never expected what was coming, was totally unsure if Craig even anticipated what he was going to do. His hand seemed to extend toward her in slow motion. His thumb grazed her cheek, and then his palm slid to the back of her neck. She saw his face looming closer. She saw his dark eyes, hooded against the sunlight.

And then his lips touched down. Softer than the whisper of a secret. His lips moved over hers, skimming soft, achingly soft, not the cocky brash kiss of a boy, nor the familiar sexual invitation of a husband. She tasted coffee and wild sweet blueberries and something indefinably dangerous. She'd been down this road before. She'd felt it before—the same deep, slow sledding into sensation, the disturbing lure of temptation, the heady rush of wonder.

Craig lifted his head. The grave frown wedged between his brows—she was sure her forehead mirrored the same frown. His lips parted at the same time hers did. She expected him to say something sensible. She certainly intended to.

Instead he muttered, "Damn it, Karen." And took her mouth again.

His palms framed the sides of her face, anchoring her still, and she suddenly couldn't breathe, couldn't think. Black lightning crackled in the air, wilder than wind, as potent as a spell of magic. One kiss tumbled into another, then another, arousing emotions that Karen could have sworn were dead and buried. She thought, *I'm dreaming this. It can't possibly be happening.*

Yet it seemed unbearably real. His tongue dived between her lips, damp and hot, seeking the intimate flavor of her. She could feel the heat pouring off his skin, the tension shooting through his muscles. He kissed her with longing; he kissed her with hunger; he kissed her as if she were a precious treasure lost, now found.

She swayed toward him, dizzy and confused, half believing that she'd been hit with a charge of that lightning. The dizziness was worse, not better, when she found his bare shoulders to hang on to. Her thighs were tucked against his then; her breasts rubbed against his chest.

"Stop it, Kara." His voice was a low harsh rasp.

She murmured, "Yes," in total honesty, total agreement.

"We can't do this."

"I know."

"This is crazy and we both know better and we're going to stop. Right now."

"Right now," she agreed, with a second to spare before his lips fused with hers again. Sunlight danced behind her closed eyes. Her neck arched, ached, when his mouth traveled down to the spinning pulse in her throat. Her lungs sucked in air, but it didn't help. Silver flushed through her veins when his hands swept the length of her spine, aggressively molding her hips closer. His breathing was rough and uneven, the pressure of his arousal an earthy, carnal warning that she couldn't mistake.

In her head, she understood this was impossible and wrong. In her head, she remembered being torn apart by hurt, specifically hurt caused by this man. And she could so easily have denied him.

But not in this life.

She'd never expected to feel it again. She thought...she'd been so sure...that the magic was lost for good, that the power to feel wonder had long died in her. It wasn't the urgency of passion that was so important. It was the feeling alive, terrifying alive, in every cell of her body.

She'd never felt it with anyone else. She'd never come close. It was only with Craig; the magic had always and only happened with Craig. And she'd never guessed—even in the years before the divorce—that he could conceivably still feel it, too.

He pulled back, looked at her face and swore. He shadow walked her toward the cabin, up the porch, the whole time muttering low, gruff warnings. The whole time spicing kisses, splicing kisses, in between those dire warnings.

The screen door refused to open by itself. He yanked it wide, and because he stopped to wrap his arms around her again, the door slapped against his behind. She pulled him inside, since he didn't seem to notice the screen. She started laughing, which earned him a fierce scowl.

"Kara, this is serious. This is terrible. This was never supposed to happen."

"So stop."

He murmured, "Maybe next Tuesday." And then, "Maybe not that soon."

He untucked her shirt, pushed aside the handfuls of cloth. He wanted the touch of her bare skin, yet he groaned when he got it. The look in his eyes tried to burn her up, but they hadn't done anything that mattered. Not yet. But the way her heart was thundering in her chest, the way he looked at her, she knew they were going to unless she stopped it, stopped him, stopped them. Quickly.

She had that choice for one long instant.

And then it was gone.

She pushed off her sandals; they lay like footprints en route to the bedroom. He fumbled with buttons. Her blouse ended up on a doorknob. Her jeans were tossed . . . somewhere.

It was darker in the bedroom, cool. Glass doors led to an open balcony, with a view of shadowy cliffs and the rocky slope of the ravine. The double bed was built into the wall, tucked under the slanted eaves. Craig ignored the sleeping bag on the floor, where he'd obviously slept in the open, and pulled her toward the bed, tumbling her down and beneath him.

His tongue sponged the fevered skin at her throat. Behind, he groped for the hooks of her plain cotton bra, thumbed them open and freed her breasts. His tongue dipped down, then his teeth. When he nipped at one tight swollen tip, her whole body arched off the bed, bucking toward him.

In a court of law, she would have produced a dozen affidavits—from her children, her parents, people she worked with—that she was responsible to a fault. Not with him. She'd never been reckless. Except with him. There was no other man who'd ever made her feel wicked and wanton, like a good girl gone bad, and

Craig had never helped her at all. He'd told her a long time ago that he wanted her to feel bad. As bad as a woman could get.

But he'd never before been so ruthless about achieving that goal.

His morning whiskers nuzzled her tender skin, courting her excitement, relishing it. His tongue laved a path of wet fire in the soft cleft between her breasts. He kissed her throat, her breasts, as if he were starving and she was the feast and it didn't make any difference to him if they ever moved off the first course.

He'd done it before. Teased her to the razor edge of sanity.

Craig must have forgotten—he'd taught her the same game.

Her hands sluiced down his ribs, over his taut flat abdomen, to the wiry nest of hair just above the snap of his jeans. The snap was tight, wouldn't give and wouldn't give, and then suddenly popped free and unleashed inches of the zipper at the same time.

She did nothing for a moment then, just looked at him. Then slowly stroked a path from the throbbing beat of his Adam's apple, down over his smooth muscled chest, down to his navel and then down again—as leisurely as a meandering stroll—to the open V of his jeans. Her fingers disappeared from sight. For one whole minute. Then two.

She saw something snap in his eyes even before he rolled her beneath him. He made a sound, half growl, half laughter, before pinning her hands. "So you wanna play rough?" he murmured.

"No."

"Yeah, you do. You love danger, Kara, you always did."

He had to free her hands to tug off his jeans. He did that fast, but he stripped off her underpants unbearably slowly, nuzzling kisses down the length of her legs before the scrap of cotton dropped off the edge of the bed.

She was bare then. So was he. And that knowledge was in his gaze that traveled back up the length of her.

Until then, she thought he was caught up in passion, startled and disarmed by a desire that had caught them both unaware. Craig had always been aggressive. In the beginning he'd scared her, with his size and his strength and his uninhibited masculine approach to sex. He didn't think, not when he was in bed. Scent, sight, touch, sounds—he was an earthy man who liked everything about a woman's body, about making love.

But she was wrong, thinking he was caught up in passion.

He wrapped her legs around him, high, almost to his waist, and then took her, filling her slowly, deeply. But there was no race to completion. His flesh was slick with sweat, his muscles wired taut, his eyes hotter than black fire.

Yet he kissed her, a kiss softer than thistledown.

And he brushed the damp hair from her temples with a tender touch.

His mouth curved in the promise of a smile. "You ready?" he whispered.

"Yes."

"I think you're expecting a roller-coaster ride, Kara. But that isn't what you're going to get."

It was something in his voice that made her shiver all over. He kissed her again, and then moved inside her. The duel and dance of lovemaking was an age-less, familiar rhythm. Yet she heard the roar of wind in her ears, a wind that wrapped around and around them, creating an intimate world of two.

No one had ever been in love but them.

No couple could have ever been as much in love as they were.

Sex was nice, but the black magic between them—the magic they created between them—had always been the spinning, wild, sweet wonder that they gave to each other. With him, she tasted that magic again. With him . . . she touched the sky.

Three

―――――

When Craig opened his eyes, the air was as still as a hush, and dusty rays of sunlight lay in patches on the plank floor. It had to be afternoon. Late afternoon. The sun only hit the cliffside bedroom for a brief stretch at the end of the day.

Groggily, very groggily, he concluded that he must have fallen asleep. Only he never usually napped. He must have been wasted to fall asleep in the middle of the day.

Slowly, still half dreaming, he remembered how he'd come to be so exhausted—and who had so unforgettably wiped him out. Sleepily he turned his head.

The atmosphere on the far side of the bed was reminiscent of a triage room in a trauma center: a frenetic overload of shock, stress and worry. Karen must have napped, too, because her cheeks still had the flush of sleep, but she definitely hadn't wakened in his own restful mood. She was curled up in a ball with her knees tucked to her chin, and she was chewing hard on a thumbnail. She looked miserable. She looked petrified.

And her eyes widened in frantic alarm when he leaned up on an elbow. "Oh, no. You're awake. Craig—it was all my fault."

He obviously needed to get a grip, fast, but it was easier said than done. His mind was still spinning pictures of how she'd looked beneath him, how fiercely and wildly they'd come together, how right—how impossibly right—it felt to have Karen back in his bed. "Kara—"

"Look . . . this kind of thing happens to lots of divorced couples. I'm not saying it's morally right, only that it happens. People get divorced, suddenly they're alone. Sexual needs don't suddenly disappear. It isn't that simple to find someone else who understands you, who knows you in bed. Strangers are scary, when at least the person you were married to—"

"Kara—" He tried again, but interrupting her was like trying to hitch a ride from a fast-moving train.

"So it happens to lots of people. Maybe they don't feel proud of themselves, but it happens."

"Okay."

"Naturally there's some guilt, but wearing a hair shirt won't help. If people crucified themselves for every mistake they made, there'd be nobody left on the planet. You can go to church. You can try your best. You can work hard to do everything right. But nobody has perfect judgment. People screw up."

At some point they must have kicked the sheet and corduroy bedspread on the floor. It occurred to Craig that nobody but his ex-wife would attempt a philosophical discussion stark naked, with a hickey on the slope of her shoulder and a second love bite on the delectably smooth curve of her right breast.

"And it's not like anyone else will ever know. It's not like we'd ever do it again," Karen said swiftly.

"No."

"Your parents live in town. My parents live in town. And the kids . . . they were precocious enough to plan our being alone here together. That's a guarantee that we could never let this happen again. More relevant, there couldn't conceivably be another opportunity with all those people around. So it was a one-time thing only and for sure. Right?"

"Right."

Her eyes suddenly shot to the curve of his neck. "Lord, did I do that to you?"

"Do what?" His hand swept up to his shoulder and behind. He felt the scratches, nothing deep enough to draw blood, but the tiny and distinctive claw marks of a lover who was wonderfully out of control. His ex-wife was a tad out of control now, too. But regretfully not in the same way.

The thumbnail snapped off between her teeth. "Craig?"

"What, honey?"

Her eyes were so luminous, so desperately unhappy. "I just want you to know—I never meant to hurt you. We've hurt each other enough. If you hate me because this happened—"

He wrapped his fingers around her wrist. "Kara...nothing you could do would ever make me hate you. Maybe there've been times I've been madder than hell, but that was anger, not hate. Never hate. And as far as making love together, I don't give a damn if it was right or wrong. I'm glad it happened and I don't regret it."

"You must," she whispered.

"I don't."

For the first time she met his eyes. "I thought you'd be angry with me."

"Who do you think initiated that first kiss? You didn't start anything. I did." His mouth twisted in the promise of a grin. "In the old days, you'd have hauled off and socked me. If you're still inclined, you've got the right."

But the only thing his ex-wife was inclined for was flight. She suddenly seemed to realize that they were holding hands, fingers twined, palms nesting together...and sharing the same pillow in a bed with neither of them clothed.

She bolted. Less than five minutes later, with her blouse buttoned haphazardly and her hair still an unbrushed tangle, she was speeding down the mountain out of sight. The excuse for her rapid flight was getting home to the children. Julie and Jon Jacob needed to be confronted about setting manipulative plans in motion—especially as concerned their parents—and Karen was not only a good mother, she was terrific at handling the awkward tricky stuff.

Getting back to the kids was a good excuse, but Craig figured Karen had a far more elemental reason for bolting.

She couldn't wait to get away from him.

He stood in the doorway until her car disappeared from sight, then raked a hand through his hair. If anyone had told him that morning that he would spend the day in bed with his ex-wife, he'd have laughed them off the map.

He wasn't laughing now.

He turned, suddenly in an all-fired rush to get away from here himself. Fast and efficiently, he stuffed a grocery bag with leftover food. He tugged on clothes, closed down windows, checked the propane supply. Back in the bedroom, he whisked off the sheet and fitted on a clean one, then started pulling on the bedspread.

In the heavy folds of the material, he found her bra.

Abruptly he forgot what a hurry he was in. He sank on the bed, holding the scrap of lingerie. It was a plain white model, cotton, 34C, no lace, no push-up wires. Nuns probably wore more seductive garments. Way back, he used to tease her about wearing good-girl bras, but Karen never flaunted her figure, never wanted strange men attracted to her looks.

The fabric smelled like her skin, with a faint trace of perfume...some soft flowery scent. Honeysuckle? She loved perfume, always wore it, but she changed it according to her mood of the day. She used to have dozens of little vials on their dresser. When she was "in the mood," it was Shalimar. When she was feeling sassy, she reached for Red. And when she was worried or stressed about something, she invariably reached for a light, cool, soothing flowery fragrance. Like honeysuckle.

So you were scared coming here, weren't you, Kara?

And you sure as hell weren't expecting to make love—ever again—with me.

His eyes squeezed closed on a flood of guilt. An old familiar friend. Heaven knew, guilt had colored his relationship with Karen from the beginning.

He still recalled, after their first disastrous experience making love, promising her earnestly and sincerely that they'd never do it again.

The promise had lasted all of three days. He'd walked her home from school, discovered her parents weren't due home until six and the next thing he knew they were in her bedroom, under a canopy bed with a bunch of stuffed animals watching their wicked antics from a corner bookshelf. Two days after that, they'd been holding hands on a simple walk in the woods, talking, just talking. An hour later they'd been searching through the bushes for their clothes.

By then he'd bought condoms, out of town where no one knew them, and had wasted a few behind a locked bathroom door because he didn't want to be fumbling like a sexually inexperienced jerk in front of Kara. He'd got down his technique, but not soon enough. They hadn't used anything the first time.

She was late.

He still remembered picking her up to go to a movie, her coming out to the car and promptly bursting into tears. She wasn't just a day late, she was a whole week late, and she was scared and shook-up. They sweated out the next two weeks, celibate as monks, as if being good now would make everything all right.

It worked. She got her period, but unfortunately both sets of parents had become worried about their relationship by then. Craig had told his dad that everything was fine. She'd told her mom that nothing was going on. Nobody had believed them. Although he'd turned eighteen that October, Karen had to wait several months before that same birthday. Possibly if they hadn't been forbidden to see each other, it wouldn't have seemed so romantic to cross the state line and elope.

Both had received scholarships to the same college that fall. Craig had promised her they'd cope. God knew how, without a penny to their names or a roof over their heads and neither set of parents speaking to them.

Yet they'd made it work. They rented an attic room on campus, got jobs, took classes, lived on peanut butter and hot sex. They had each other. They didn't care about anything else. They had a love that would never die.

But condoms had failed them when Karen was nineteen. Jonathan Jacob came along, then Julie the next year. Kara dropped out of school, but she never seemed to mind. She loved being a mom, loved him, loved life. And God knew, he'd have killed for her.

Unfortunately the romantic notion of killing for his true love wasn't an option on the menu. Formula was more expensive than peanut butter. Hot sex didn't pay the rent. Kara got a job typing. He couldn't drop out of college—not and support them decently for the long-term—but he took a second part-time job.

And that was the last time he saw his wife for almost a dozen years.

Craig stared blindly at the slanted beam ceiling. Obviously that was an exaggeration. He *saw* her. He lived with her. He slept with her. They'd raised two children together. But he'd lost Kara somewhere during that time. And still—damnation!—had no idea how.

All those years guilt had eaten him alive. He was responsible for seducing Kara before she was really ready. He was responsible for coaxing her into marriage when they were both too young. He was responsible for their being broke. He was responsible . . . for everything. He was always the one who'd led them into trouble, and he had to make it right for her.

Only, he thought he had.

The next time he looked up, they had a house in the suburbs, he was marketing vice president for Hytech, the kids were finally old enough to give them some free time, and he was making money hand over fist. They should have been happy. Instead they fought. Nasty, ugly, sniping fights. Over stupid things like who did the lawn, or who brought home the cleaning, or what idiotic channel they watched on TV.

The magic wasn't just gone.

It had been stomped to death.

Eventually he had to face it—Karen just plain didn't love him anymore. The divorce hadn't hurt. Living together had been unbearable—the divorce was a legal relief from pain, and he'd gone on with his life.

Or thought he had. *If the magic was so stomped dead, then what happened this morning, Craig Reardon? What happened to her? What happened to you?*

And more relevant, what are you going to do about it?

The following Wednesday, Karen left work at the dot of five and arrived home early. Heading into the house, she noted the freshly mowed lawn and the trash neatly stacked for tomorrow's pickup. Jon Jacob's doing. Inside the lemon-and-white kitchen, she found clean counters, no dirty dishes and a pot of sloppy joes simmering on the stove. Julie's doing.

All week, both children could have auditioned for starring roles as model teenagers. Karen slipped off her spectator pumps and red blazer, musing that motherhood was a constant hit-or-miss process of finding the right buttons to push.

She hadn't yelled at them for their matchmaking attempt with her and Craig. There had been no punishment, no scolding. She simply told them that she loved them and understood their feelings—most kids with divorced parents wanted their family reunited. She was sorry they had mistakenly hoped a reconciliation could happen. It wouldn't. Couldn't. To try something like that again was to risk embarrassing and hurting their father.

That was all she'd said, but both kids had looked stricken. Apparently it had never occurred to either of them that their matchmaking scheme might have hurt their father.

The house had been clean every day since and her monsters had transformed into angels.

Karen didn't like laying guilt trips on the kids—it went against her whole style of parenting—but conceivably once in fifteen years was excusable. Neither, she sincerely believed, were considering any alternative matchmaking schemes.

It mattered. She wasn't yet sure if she'd survived their first one.

"Mom! You're home early!"

Karen whirled around. "Hi, sweetheart. Thanks for
getting dinner started. You're a peach." She swept up
her youngest for a quick hug, thinking that Julie was
getting impossibly beautiful. She had her father's
striking coloring—the same tawny hair and dark eyes.
Boys had been calling for a year now, but so far Julie
hadn't given any of them the time of day, which was
more than okay by Karen. "How was school?"

"Boring."

Karen would probably have suffered shock if the
response had been anything else. "You finding your
classes okay? Got any good teachers?" The kids had
just gone back to school this week. Her daughter
earned high honors and, although she wouldn't admit it at the point of a dagger, loved school.

"Everything's okay," Julie said impatiently, and
then hesitated. "Mom, something happened."

"What?"

"I was *trying* to help you. So when I came home, I
put in a wash."

"And?"

"And that cocoa-colored cotton sweater that you
love so much... I didn't know you couldn't dry it. I
thought I'd read the labels on everything—"

"Mmm. What size did it end up?"

"Maybe it'd fit on a poodle. A small poodle.
Cripes, I'm sorry."

"No sweat. What's a sweater?" Possibly there were
a few unfortunate repercussions to having temporarily ideal, perfect, overhelpful teenagers. Karen didn't
care. As long as the kids harbored no more ridiculous
hopes about her and Craig getting back together,
Karen wouldn't care if she lost her whole wardrobe.

"Hey, Mom. You're home."

Again, she spun around. Jon dutifully bent down for his hug. For about three years, he'd shunned any expression of affection coming from a female, including his mother. He'd grown out of that, thank heavens. Around the time he'd towered over her by five inches, he seemed to decide that hugs were something mothers did and he was man enough to be tolerant.

"Don't tell me. You're starving. Dinner will be ready in two shakes. School go okay? Homework?"

"Homework's all done." He rolled his eyes when she placed a shocked hand over her heart. "I also did the lawn."

"I know. I saw, and thanks, shorty."

"Gram called. She wants us over to dinner on Friday. And I talked to Fitz about a part-time job after school."

Karen wasn't so sure about that job. Jon Jacobs had to work for a *B* average without adding extra pressures to his plate, but his only dream in life right now was making money. He wanted a car. His own car. He wanted it more than he wanted air to breathe.

"Come on, Mom. I can handle it. At least lemme try. If my grades slip, I can always quit."

"We'll talk about it," Karen promised him.

Dinner was typically fast, messy and rambunctious. Jon apparently had a new girlfriend. Julie needled him—hard. A glass of milk spilled. Both kids claimed an allergy to squash, similar to the allergy they still claimed to every vegetable. The phone rang three times—twice for Julie. Boys, Karen guessed, because her daughter turned brick red and couldn't wait to get off the phone. And there was one call for Jon that he took with his hand jammed in his jeans pocket and his voice artificially lowered to a baritone. It had to be a girl. The new girl.

Jon showed a paternally inherited tendency toward an overactive libido that worried Karen, but not too much. When her son stayed interested in one girl for longer than a week, then she figured she could start worrying in earnest.

She left them bickering over dishes, went to the living room and flicked on the TV news. As she sat curled up in a corner of the couch, Dan Rather predictably came up with a full quota of wars, drugs and crime. She couldn't seem to pay attention.

It had been an unusually good week, she thought. Temporary guilt trip or not, the kids were both on an even keel, happy, busy. Her work had rarely gone better. Jim, the CEO of Macalvey's and her boss, had sprung for a raise on Monday. It had been a long climb up from a keypuncher in the word-processing pool to his personal administrative assistant. Jim was sixty-three and could have been the old-fashioned kind of boss who expected her to make the coffee. Instead, over the years, he'd pushed her into projects she was afraid of and responsibilities she couldn't cope with. Now he claimed she could run the place without him, which was true. But the extra raise had been an unexpected surprise.

So the whole week had been golden, Karen mentally repeated to herself. With one teensy exception. Her nerves were in shreds. She was antsy enough to climb the walls.

A restless breeze sifted through the filmy curtains. She glanced around the room with a frustrated frown. Upstairs, there were three bedrooms. Downstairs was the lemon-and-white kitchen, a utility room, the kids' giant den and this—the small, square living room that was supposed to be her sanctuary, her oasis, the one place where she could catch a moment of peaceful quiet when she needed to.

The carpet was cream, the general color scheme toast and salmon, but beyond that the room was an uncoordinated hodgepodge. The salmon pottery was contemporary Native American in style, while the swaybacked ivory love seat was a century old. A surrealistic mountain landscape, all corals and browns, hung over a carved spiral table that had been made in Boston in Revolutionary times. The peach couch was new. The globed lamp with hanging prisms had been her great-grandmother's.

Karen knew the room reflected her pitiful decorating taste and didn't give a damn. After the divorce, the room had reminded her of Craig every time she walked in it. Like a ferret, she'd collected the things she loved around her. It worked for her. It didn't have to work for anyone else.

Only nothing was successfully calming her edginess tonight. *You're okay.* The phrase had popped in her mind a dozen times since Saturday, as if a little genie in her head was determined to reassure her. *Everything's normal. The kids, the house, work. You're doing everything the same way you always do. Your whole world didn't shatter last Saturday. You're okay.*

She leaned back her head, determined to relax, when the doorbell rang. With a grimace she sprang off the couch and padded in stocking feet to the door. The boy on the other side reached a lanky six feet, had three whiskers growing on his chin and looked sheepishly mortified at having bothered her. "He's either in the kitchen or the den, Rog," she said.

Roger promptly disappeared in search of her son.

Six minutes later, the bell buzzed again. Karen uncurled from the couch—again—to greet the hooker at the door. At least, the girl had enough makeup to pass for the working trade. Her tank top was tight and brazenly worn without a bra, and Karen noted the new hole in her ear. That made four.

"Julie's either in the kitchen or the den," she said.

"She's probably busy."

"She's not busy."

"I don't want to bother her."

Karen suppressed a sigh. One of these days she was going to figure out Martha. How could a girl who wore such outlandish attire be such a painfully insecure introvert? "She'll be glad you're here, honey," Karen said soothingly. "Come on in."

Martha, like Rog, obediently trotted down the hall.

She'd just—*just*—settled back on the couch when the doorbell rang yet again. So, she thought, it was going to be one of those nights. Teenagers clustered closer than grapes. Other parents had the brains to realize how fast a group of teenagers could decimate a house. Nobody wanted them. Nobody in their right mind would open up their home as a place to hang out, and Karen knew darn well every parent in the neighborhood had her pegged as a sucker.

Which she was. Mentally worrying whether she had enough pop and potato chips to last the evening—it was a foolish worry, there was never enough—she crossed the room to answer the door for the third time.

"They're either in the kitchen or the—" She stopped midsentence.

It wasn't an overgrown awkward teenager in the doorway this time, but an intimidatingly tall man in a gray striped business suit.

All the saliva dried in her mouth. Her tongue felt thick, and the pulse in her throat was suddenly beating, beating, beating. Her ex-husband, she guessed, must have come straight from work, because he was still wearing a tie and his eyes looked worn and tired. His gaze whisked the length of her, taking in her slim navy skirt and tuxedo-pleated white blouse, but his expression reflected no special emotion. If anything, he seemed preoccupied.

"I'm sorry, Karen. I know I should have called. But I got away from work earlier than I expected for the first time all week, and I promised you that I'd talk with the kids."

"It doesn't matter about calling first. But as far as the children, I already talked to them."

"I know. Or I guessed that you had. But you get stuck more than I do when there's a problem, and this is one where I think we should both be involved. Are they home?"

Craig disappeared, just like the others, in the direction of the kitchen.

Karen never moved from the doorway. The intrusion of an adult—any adult—into a teenage gathering had predictable results. Moments later, Roger ambled down the hall and only tripped once on his way out the door. He was quickly followed by Martha. Both said a swift, "Catch you later, Ma."

Karen was thirty-six, not one hundred and ten, and reliably ruffled for the epitaph of "Ma" that the kids teased her with. Tonight she didn't take the bait. Even minutes after the kids were out of sight, she was still standing frozen in the door. The imaginary little genie in her head kept repeating, *You're okay, Karen. You're okay.*

Only, she wasn't okay. She hadn't been remotely okay since making love with Craig, and she had been frantically worried all week about facing him again. She assumed it would be difficult. She assumed there would be heavy, awkward emotional vibrations between them . . . and there certainly were. For her. For her, an innocuous September evening had suddenly electrified. Her heart was thumping harder than a tail-wagging dog. Blood was shooting straight to her head.

Apparently her ex-husband had none of those ridiculous problems. How many zillions of times had he walked in, shared a few seconds of conversation with her and then disappeared to be with the children? Nothing was different. Last Saturday might never have happened. She was thankful and relieved that making love had obviously meant nothing important to him.

Enormously relieved and deliriously thankful, she told herself firmly. Lord! The potential repercussions, if either of them still cared, could have been disastrous—for the kids, for her, for them. It wasn't as if she'd built up any foolish, false hopes from that one encounter. Sex was just . . . sex. Making love one last time changed nothing at all. They'd burned the last of their emotional bridges with the divorce. There was no going back.

And any second now, Karen told herself, any second now, the huge swelling lump in her throat was going to disappear.

Four

_____

Karen never intended to eavesdrop. She moved away from the door, and too restless to settle in front of the television, wandered down the hall to fetch the paperback lying on the Parsons table. It wasn't her fault that voices carried clearly from the open door of the kitchen. She meant to walk away—Craig had every right to talk privately with the kids—but the subject of their conversation was impossible to ignore.

Both children knew they could occasionally pull the wool over her eyes. They rarely tried that nonsense with their father. Craig's style of parenting was blunt and own-up honest, and as Karen might have guessed, he was forcing the children to talk about their feelings. En route, he was definitely expressing his own.

If Karen had any lingering hopes that making love had changed anything between them, listening to her ex-husband was as sure a cure as a dentist's drill for a cavity.

"Look, Dad, we're sorry. We never meant to hurt you or Mom."

"You owe an apology to your mother, not me. All I want is some straight answers from both of you. You concocted quite a scheme to get your mother and me together at the cabin. Obviously you two had a purpose in mind. What exactly did you want—or think— was going to happen?"

Karen heard their son uneasily clear his throat. "We just figured if there was somebody else in the picture—like a guy for Mom, or some girl she thought you were seeing—that you two would realize you still cared about each other."

Julie burst in, "And you jumped, Dad. You *know* you did. I saw your face when I told you Mom might be in trouble—"

"And Mom—when I told Mom you had a girl, she almost had a stroke. I mean, you guys still *do* care about each other—"

Craig quietly interrupted. "So you discovered that your mother and I still have feelings for each other. You thought this was big news? You thought this would be some miraculous revelation for the two of us?"

"Dad—"

"Dad—"

"Julie, you led me to believe that your mother was in trouble. And, Jon, you laid an even heavier scene on your mother. So, yes, we both 'jumped.' Just because two people are divorced doesn't mean that they stop feeling all concern for each other."

"But Mason's parents are divorced." Jon's voice crackled with nerves. "They can't even be in the same room without yelling. You and Mom were never mean to each other like that."

"Which means absolutely nothing, Son. People get divorced for different reasons, and handle it in different ways." Craig's tone had the rough burr of authority. "I don't want to see either one of you—ever—put your mother through anything like that again. You embarrassed and upset her, and interfered in something that you know nothing about." His voice gentled. "Listen. Both of you. Did you think we went through a divorce for nothing? Did you think that your mother and I would have put ourselves through that—or you two through that—if we could conceivably have made it work between us?"

Karen looked down to find her hands wrapped so tightly around the paperback that her knuckles were white. Craig had always had the gift for hitting a nail on the head, she thought bleakly.

What happened between them on Saturday may have emotionally knocked her for six, but that crazy moment in time shouldn't have blindsided her to past history. They'd moved their share of heaven and earth before. It hadn't helped. They'd loved each other. That hadn't helped, either. Nothing had helped. They simply couldn't make the relationship work.

Wanting—suddenly, fiercely—to disappear from sight, she half turned. Seconds too late. Craig strode through the door and caught her standing there.

Color shot to her cheeks. Feeling guilty as a shoplifter, she showed him the paperback. "I was just—"

He put a finger to his lips, then silently steered her toward the front door. Once outside, she paused on the front steps, but he shook his head and kept going. Karen understood that he wanted to talk away from the children's hearing, but she had no shoes on. And he was whipping across the lawn toward the garage at a racing pace.

She compressed her lips and padded after him, mentally writing off her pair of stockings to her own need for speed. She assumed he wanted to affirm that they were presenting a united parental front to the kids. That shouldn't take four seconds. The instant he left, she intended to take her battered emotions upstairs, pour a gallon of fragrance into a hot soaking bath and wallow for a good long hour. Maybe two. She'd feel better then.

Truthfully, she'd bet gold that her miserable mood would begin to improve the moment her ex-husband was gone from her sight. Maybe there was a way to cut a four-second conversation down to three.

A tiny stick caught between her stocking toes. Hopping, she freed it and then glanced up. "Craig, for heaven's sake—"

She couldn't believe it. He disappeared behind the corner of the garage. There was nothing back there but the fall's stack of firewood, a forgotten bicycle tire and ankle-high weeds. It took a minute for her to catch up. She had to gingerly tiptoe through the sawdust and wood chips.

When he swiveled around, his gaze shot instantly to her feet. "You don't have any shoes on," he observed.

No one, but no one, could exasperate her faster than her ex-husband. "Reardon! Was I supposed to guess that you planned to talk behind the garage?"

"I didn't exactly plan it. I just wanted to go someplace where the kids wouldn't know where we were for a few minutes."

He'd certainly accomplished that. Neither Jon nor Julie would conceivably guess that their dual set of responsible parents were hiding behind the wood stack. Karen's sense of humor surfaced, then faded abruptly. "I heard what you told them, and I agree with how you handled it. You made very sure they had no more illusions about our getting back together again."

The sun was setting fast, and Craig's expression was shadowed in the blurry light. "I didn't want them thinking up any more matchmaking schemes. Not just for our sakes, Kara. For theirs."

"Like I said—I completely agree. They were hurt enough when we split up."

"They shouldn't be involved in our problems."

She nodded, for once on a perfect wavelength with her ex-husband, and she saw Craig lift his arms. She saw, but it never crossed her mind that he was reaching for her until the horse was already out of the barn. His hands clutched her shoulders and drew her up on tiptoe. He angled his head, blocking her view of the sunset red sky, and then his mouth latched on hers, locked on hers, as if a kiss between them couldn't wait any longer.

Thoughts shredded through her mind like confetti. She'd thought that the kids were the only thing on his mind. She'd thought he'd written off their lovemaking on Saturday as the insane, mistaken, irresponsible encounter that it was. And it didn't matter if she was hurt. She'd counted on Craig—to be wiser than she was.

Yet there was no wisdom in his kiss. She tasted hunger, desperation, a searching in the harsh pressure of his mouth. She saw the same emotions in his luminous dark eyes. It was like Saturday. Only worse. The feel of his hands, urgent and arousing, the intimate flavor of his tongue, the rush and strain and secret excitement from being this close. . . .

A trembling started from deep inside her. Fear, but a delicious fear, like being poised on the tip of a high dive with a mirror-black lake below. So quickly, so impossibly quickly, she could be immersed in that water, in so far, down so deep that she might never surface again. Maybe she'd never breathe again.

She felt as if she'd never breathe again if he stopped kissing her. "Damn it, Kara." She heard him, but his voice was the drug of a caress, whiskey hoarse and low. His lips pleated down her throat, then back, behind the lobe of her ear. "Be good," he scolded, but he was the one being wicked. He knew the shell of her ear was painfully sensitive, and his hands opened, sliding possessively down her spine to the curve of her hips. Like lightning was drawn to water, she surged against him. He was harder than steel. Hot steel. And God forgive her, but the fire shooting through her veins was just as hot. "Karen."

He gripped her shoulders and reared back his head. Air hissed out of his lungs in a frustrated whoosh.

Shock snapped her back to reality. What couldn't happen again—what couldn't, shouldn't, was never supposed to happen again—had. A sudden silence hung between them with electric volatility. She saw the raw dark passion in his eyes; she saw his jaw muscle clench in a fierce bid for control. But she didn't know him as well as she once had. At that precise instant, Karen was terrified to realize that possibly she'd never known him at all.

"You're shaking," he said gruffly.

She nodded. It would be pretty ridiculous to deny it. Her knees had the tensile strength of overcooked pasta.

"Scared?"

She nodded again, just as numbly.

"You're not the only one." His thumb brushed her cheek, gently, softly, and then he dropped his hands and motioned to the short stack of logs. "How about if you sit there—" he backed up to the white-sided garage "—and I stand here. And we both keep that nice, safe distance between us until we've talked this out."

His dry attempt at humor was a little forced, but Karen was more than willing to put that nice, safe distance between them. She sank on the edge of a sturdy log and took a deep breath. "Craig... I don't understand what's going on here."

"You think I do?"

"But you started this. Deliberately. It wasn't like Saturday—it wasn't an impulse. You deliberately kissed me."

"Yes. Because I wanted to know if Saturday was something I daydreamed in some fantasy, or whether what happened between us was real." He rolled his shoulders against the rough-sided wall, yanked his tie loose. "Don't tell me you didn't want to know the same thing, Kara. I saw the way you looked at me when I first walked in the house."

"I thought... that you'd forgotten it, put it out of your mind."

"Honey, I'd need a lobotomy to forget it." Their eyes met, his spiced with honesty and dark humor. Yet he studied her face with lancing intensity. "If I asked you a question, would you answer it straight? No thinking about it, no hedging, just... straight?"

She waited, unsure what was coming.

Again Craig's eyes fused with hers. "I want to know what went wrong. What *really* went wrong between us, because I'll be damned if I'm sure I ever knew."

Her fingers suddenly dug into the rough bark of the log. "Come on, Craig. Maybe we managed to keep it from the kids, but we were fighting like cats and dogs, sniping at each other, drawing blood every time we turned around."

"I *know* that. I remember the anger. But I'm not sure I knew—if I ever knew—why you were so mad at me."

"That anger was a two-way street," she reminded him. "It wasn't just me."

"Okay. But right now all I'm interested in is what *you* felt."

She felt the bark scrape against her tender palms, saw the sunset bleeding red through the straggly border hedges. Other women seemed to find it easy and natural to talk about emotions. Not her. She'd dammed up, clammed up, after the divorce. To expose the old wounding hurts... she couldn't.

"Kara? Just try, okay? Just try and talk to me. I don't want to hurt you. But I need to understand."

Maybe if he'd demanded, she could have shut him down. But his voice was as quiet as pain, and that need to understand...she'd also felt it. Her heart, too, had spent dark hours in a limbo of unanswered questions and hurts that refused to heal. She lifted a hand in a helpless gesture, not looking at him, conscious that her voice was thickening with unshed tears. "It wasn't one thing. It was a million things that built up and built up and built up."

Surprising her, upsetting her, it all poured out like a pent-up dam. "I always put you and the children first. That's what I *wanted* to do—you never forced me...but everything I personally wanted was always put on hold. You got your degree, your education, but I never got mine. The only job I could get was typing, and, yes, I worked myself up the ranks, but that took so many years...all those years when I was working full-time and trying to be a good mom and taking care of the house, scrimping and saving and you—you never seemed to notice. Or you stopped noticing. Stopped caring. I felt used and taken for granted. Your career skyrocketed—your whole life took off—while I was still back at the ranch, the old-fashioned wife behind the scenes, as boring and dull as an old habit."

Craig let out a succinct expletive. "Why the hell didn't you tell me any of this before?"

"I told you. I told you in a dozen ways, a hundred ways," she said fiercely.

"The hell you did—and don't you dare cry. This is the first time you've talked to me in years. Really talked to me. Honestly talked to me. Apparently you expected me to guess how you felt as if I were some kind of mind reader—"

"No." Tears matted her eyelashes, but she took a long cleansing breath. It was hard, this kind of sharing. She'd rather walk on fire. But they'd come this far, and if Craig was intent on honesty, she suddenly wanted the air cleared between them just as much. "No, I never thought you were a mind reader," she said wearily, "but I'll be damned if I know how a woman's supposed to tell a man who's breaking her heart that he's breaking her heart. There was nothing to say, Craig. Not once you stopped caring."

"Kara?"

"What?"

"I was furious with you. And hurt. But I never stopped caring." He rubbed a hand over his eyes, then shook his head. Slowly, gruffly, he exposed his own old wounds.

"You never seemed to realize how hard I was working, how hard I was trying to be a success in your eyes. I was the one who got you in trouble, sunshine. I was always the one who got us in trouble. From where I sat—I had to make that right. Only, by the time I had my whole act together, you seemed to have totally lost interest. You were always busy with a hundred other things. We came together in bed, but it was like fire and smoke. A fast flame, a burn up, and then you were too busy to give me the time of day. I was trying so hard to make so many things up to you—"

She let out a short expletive. "For cripes' sake, Craig. You never needed to make anything up to me. Where did you ever get such an idea? And why—long,

long before this—didn't you ever tell me how you felt?"

Craig said dryly, deliberately, "I thought I had. In a dozen ways, a hundred ways."

Karen heard the echo of her own words and lifted her head. The red ball of sun had disappeared from sight. Shadows darkened the still evening and the temperature was dropping fast, a harbinger of fall. She heard a door slam somewhere, a car's engine misfire on the road, a neighbor calling for her cat. Lights were popping on in the house. Jon and Julie could come looking for them at any time.

Yet she couldn't look away from Craig's eyes. There were years between them, a history of mistakes and a history of hurt, but also a history of love. Possibly they could never have hurt each other so badly if they hadn't loved so fiercely.

Karen had never guessed that his drive and preoccupation and ruthless climb to the top had been linked to her, that he'd doubted, ever, being a success in her eyes. It shamed her, that she had been so insensitive. And it frightened her, that she could know so little about the man she had loved with her entire heart and soul.

"I never meant to hurt you," she said softly.

"I never meant to hurt you, either." Emotion shone in his eyes. "But I also never expected to make love with you again, Kara. I thought it was gone. I thought it was lost. I thought you had no feelings left for me at all—"

"We can't go back."

"You think I want to?"

She searched his face. "No. But everything is completely different now."

"I know that."

"The kids—they already have ideas about getting us back together. They'd be confused and upset all over again if we started seeing each other and the relationship didn't work." She shook her head. "When we were seventeen, we had an excuse for being impulsive and irresponsible. Now there are other people affected by what we do. We can't take chances like that again."

"Of course we can't."

"There's nothing to do. Nothing we *can* do. Both of us have too many unshakable responsibilities. And the kids—privacy would be completely impossible."

Craig nodded. "So we ignore it."

"Yes."

"There's no other choice."

"Exactly."

"It sounds great in theory, Kara. Particularly when you're three feet away." Even in the shadows, she could see the glint of wry, dry masculine humor in his eyes. "How about if you come here. Close. So you can show me how good we're gonna be at ignoring this tiny little forest fire between us."

Karen had bypassed the cooking sherry and went straight for the dusty bottle of bourbon she kept around for holidays. Downstairs—once the kids were in bed—she'd tipped the bottle into a nice, tall water glass. The first sip had trickled down her throat with the sting of a burn, but she intended to level if.

She had to work tomorrow, which meant she *had* to sleep.

Her toe flicked off the water faucet. The water in the tub was filled to the brim, and scented with her entire supply of damask rose. Flowery scents always relaxed her, always soothed her. Always. And rose was a subtle, soft, alluring scent.

A lump suddenly clogged in her throat. A hundred years ago, Craig had brought her tea roses. Back then, they were struggling on a hamburger budget. Their entire decor was early attic. The electric, phone and heating bills were always in arrears. She felt guilty if she bought a new lipstick. His collars were all frayed. And the jerk, her damned jerk of a new husband, had bought her roses.

Not one, but a whole extravagant dozen.

She'd desperately loved those roses. They hadn't been red but a pale, pale yellow, their color as subtle and precious as their fragrance. She'd put them in a water glass, because she had no vase. At first the buds had been closed and tight, but over days the petals had burst open for light and sun.

Even thinking about those roses made her ache, made her want, made her love him all over again.

Drink, Karen. Heaven knows something has to give you a dose of reality. Drink. Drink.

She took another thick gulp of bourbon, and sank deeper in the tub water. Her skin was shriveling like a wrinkled plum, but she wasn't ready to get out yet.

The magic—that old black devil magic—was between them again. She knew it. He knew it. Julie and Jon had stood out on the front porch, calling, *"Mom?*

Dad?'' And still the devil in the stark gray suit hadn't let her go, wouldn't let her go, the look in his eyes more powerful than a magnet.

"I don't know you anymore," he'd admitted.

"And I don't know you."

"It would be deep waters, Kara. With no guarantee of a life buoy in sight. We failed before. Even loving each other, we failed before."

She'd nodded fiercely.

She remembered nodding fiercely.

"But what if we tried? Just between you and me. If we were careful no one else was involved, no one else knew." He picked his words carefully. "No expectations. Both of us are too smart to build up unrealistic expectations. But I would honestly like to know who you are now. I just . . . want to see you, talk with you. What terrible harm could happen if we just got to know each other again?"

Outside, at that instant, his suggestion had made so much sense to Karen. When their relationship had started going wrong, she'd lost more than a husband. She'd lost her best friend. It seemed to be all he was asking for—to discover if it was possible that they could still be friends again.

She swallowed a third sip of bourbon, but the alcohol was worthless. Adrenaline was pumping through her veins faster than shooting rockets. She could taste the danger. She could taste the flavor of too many old hurts. She could taste the memory of almost losing her soul the last time they'd failed.

Foolishly—thinking with her heart, not her head—she'd agreed to see him again.

But she was scared. Scared that they'd never manage to be friends again. And even more scared that they would.

Five

Karen fluffed the bed pillows, propped a pair of reading glasses on her nose and reached for the paperback on her nightstand. It was almost midnight. She was on page two when a heartrending shriek echoed from below.

An entire herd of elephants pounded up the stairs. Seconds later, the herd thundered down again. A second glass-shattering shriek echoed two floors, followed by giggles. Secret, exuberant, excited giggles. The VCR volume rose to deafening pitch, then quit. Rock and roll suddenly blared from the stereo in the den, loud enough to make the dead glad they were dead.

Julie had said, "You don't mind if I have a few girls over on Saturday night, do you, Mom? We'll be real quiet, I promise. You won't even know we're there."

Karen turned another page. In another hour, she figured, she'd exert control over the bedlam. Sooner than that was wasted breath. Until the girls ran off some of that incredible teenage energy, they were simply incapable of settling down.

As she reached down to scratch an itch on her right toe, she heard a sound. A peculiar sound, like a quick pelt of hail on the windows. The midnight sky was cloudless and clear.

Yet she heard the strange noise again. With a frown, she scooched to the edge of the double bed and pushed aside the cream-fringed curtains. The window reflected her scrubbed face and oldest blue sweatshirt, but nothing outside—not with the light shining behind her.

She switched off the lamp and peered out again. A handful of dirt splatted on the window at a level with her nose. She jerked back reflexively, then heaved an exasperated sigh. She'd been tolerant. She'd been understanding. And she absolutely hated getting painted as the Wicked Witch of the West, but there were a few rules the girls knew better than to break. Horseplay outside, this late at night, was one of them.

She flipped the window lock and threw open the sash, mentally gearing up to deliver a maternal scold...only there were no cavorting fifteen-year-old girls below.

Enough downstairs lights reflected outside that she could make out the single figure of a man. He was standing in the frost-tipped grass with his hands on his hips.

Fear never crossed her mind. Even in the dark, he was a heckuva good-looking—and familiar—boogey-

man. Dressed in dark clothes, a black sweatshirt
and jeans, his long, broad-shouldered frame cast a
formidable shadow. His face was tilted toward the
window—lean jaw, Apache-black eyes, his hair unbrushed in a disreputably tawny rumple.

Butterflies fluttered in her stomach, not a few but
an entire flock of them. The sensation of déjà vu was
so strong that for an instant Karen thought she was
seventeen again, grounded in her room, forbidden to
see Craig...yet he'd come, pelting dirt at her window, defying his parents and her parents and anybody else who dared keep her from him. She'd been
Rapunzel stuck in the tower. He'd been her dark
knight.

She shook off the déjà vu sensation. It was no boy
below, but a grown man. A dangerous grown man,
who had infested her dreams with his earthy sensuality and a hope she was afraid to believe in. She hadn't
slept well in two weeks because of him. She felt frag-
ile and confused because of him. He'd busted her
whole sense of balance, and now he thought she'd be
happy to see him?

He must not have spotted her yet, because he
abruptly leaned down. She had visions of him scooping up another handful of black dirt from her flower
bed.

Hurriedly she leaned over the sill. "Pssst!" she
hissed.

He straightened. His dark eyes found her in the
shadowed sill. He shot her a hell-raising grin, white
teeth against a roguish tan, the kind of grin that used
to push the accelerator of her nerves straight to the
floor.

Damnation. It still did. But Craig didn't necessarily need to know that her toes were curling. "Are you crazy, Reardon? Are you plumb-nuts certifiable? If you wanted to come in, why didn't you just use the door?"

"For the obvious reason, Kara. I didn't want to come in. I wanted you to come down."

"Down?"

"Down. Here. Outside. And for Pete's sake, hurry up before anyone sees you."

Karen wasn't about to do any such thing—at least without a reason why—but he disappeared into the shadows before she had the chance to demand an explanation. Exasperated, she pushed down the window and glanced at herself. After a shower, she'd pulled on her oldest sweats. The pants bagged in the knees and the sweatshirt had old, familiar, comfortable holes. No underwear, no shoes, no makeup. Chaperoning a gaggle of girls didn't exactly call for formal dress.

And she was too old, she told herself, *much* too old to sneak outside to meet a man in the middle of the night like some immature, foolhardy teenager.

But she *was* curious about what he wanted.

Badly, naggingly, nail-bitingly curious.

Feeling uneasy, feeling foolish, she slipped on sneakers, tiptoed to the top of the stairs and peeked over the banister. Rolled-up sleeping bags landscaped the front hall. Someone was in the kitchen; she heard the refrigerator door open and slam closed. But the major source of noise was coming from the den—giggles and laughter and rock and roll; the girls were dancing.

The coast to the front door was temporarily clear.

I'll only be gone a couple of minutes, she promised herself. Yet when she slipped outside, there was no sign of Craig. The night air was crisp and chill. Trees lined the neatly trimmed lawns, silvery yellow under the streetlights, but the night was as still as a tomb and ghostly quiet. She rubbed her arms nervously.

Maybe she'd taken too long and he'd left? Craig only lived three blocks away. At the time of the divorce, it was another thing their attorneys had argued with them about—Craig buying a house so close to hers. But they shared mutual custody. This way the kids could bike or walk the distance between houses, and did all the time.

But there were no kids on the streets now—not theirs or anyone else's. Karen rubbed her arms harder, and then suddenly spotted the back end of his white Cherokee, parked on the road but half-hidden behind her neighbor's white picket fence. She sprinted toward it, her sneakers soaking in the crunchy grass, unsure why she was hurrying, even less sure of the wisdom of meeting him at all.

Yet as she neared the truck, the passenger door of the Cherokee opened as if by magic, and she suddenly found herself starting to chuckle. A big hand extended, fingers cupped, frantically motioning her inside.

"It took you long enough. For cripes' sake, get in here before any of them find us."

"Before any of who?"

"The kids." Craig slumped back against the driver door and cocked one foot on the seat. "The noise level at my house threatens true deafness—which is all your fault. If you hadn't agreed to having some cocka-mamy pajama party, Jon would never have come over with the long face and the big line about how long it'd been since he'd had the guys over. I still don't believe I got suckered in—get in, get in.''

"I—"

Craig could see she was nervous. So was he, but he didn't want her to know it. "It occurred to me that we temporarily had the same problem—no peace, no privacy and no place to go. It seems to me I remember complaining about this problem when I was seventeen. Feels like sneaking out all over again, doesn't it?''

"Worse," she admitted with a chuckle. She folded in and latched the door, but not tightly. She didn't have her physical act together enough to pay much attention. Her eyes sought his in the darkness, as wary as a lamb with a wolf.

She'd come this far—as he'd hoped, his staging an impromptu encounter in the middle of the night had tickled her curiosity and sense of humor. But now he could see she wasn't so sure about what she'd signed up for. Her shoulders were hunched together and tense. Her hands didn't know what to do with themselves. "I really shouldn't leave the girls alone for long—''

"Fifteen minutes max, I figured, as far as trusting the boys." Actually the boys were being good as gold, quietly playing poker, and he'd told Jon Jacob that a call to his sister would reach him. But Karen looked reassured when she heard that short time limit. At least she leaned back against the seat and tucked a leg under her, no longer looking quite so ready to fly.

"What's that smell?" she queried.

"Pizza. And a couple cans of pop stolen from the kids' stash. You hungry?" He shot her a dark look as he reached in the back seat. "You'd *better* be hungry. I can't eat this whole thing alone. Extra cheese, ham, peppers and a million black olives—"

"Olives?"

"It was the only pizza left over that the boys didn't decimate," Craig said dryly. A total lie. He'd threatened the gang with murder if they touched it. "Must have been the olives." He fluttered a dozen napkins in her lap, then reached for the awkward cardboard box. "No silverware. I didn't think that far ahead. It just occurred to me on the spur of the moment that you might need a few minutes' freedom from bedlam as much as I did."

"Olives," she said again. Much more weakly.

She'd always loved the suckers. Black olives, not green. Once, at three in the morning, when she was pregnant with Jon Jacob, Craig had to search the whole damn college town for a store that was still open *and* that sold black olives. When he got home, she'd leveled the entire jar.

"Maybe one slice," she said primly.

She devoured four, scrunched up on the seat, dangling the strings of cheese around her fingers and getting pizza crumbs all over his truck.

Too late, Craig remembered that no one had ever made him laugh like Kara. She swore at him when he accused her of greed. When a car drove by, they ducked like kids afraid of getting caught. She laughed—and kept laughing—when a fat green pepper plopped in his lap.

They didn't talk about kids or family or work. They just . . . talked. About the shape of the moon. About a scrawny calico tomcat who'd followed her home once. About how hopeless they both were at photography. She'd taken a class in Chinese history—he had no idea she'd developed that interest. She had no idea that he'd been dabbling with local politics.

Neither lingered on any one subject. Neither tried. Karen seemed to naturally come up with more topics than he did, but that was understandable. By then his mind was reeling, distracted.

He'd convinced himself that he had ethical, honest, logical reasons for seeing her again. Two weeks before, passion had flamed between them like the spontaneous combustion of a single match in a dry forest. The same explosive magic had seeped—sneaked—into the kiss in her backyard.

Craig thought he understood what was happening. They'd split up because they were driving each other crazy. The divorce had successfully stopped that cycle of hurt, but ultimately it was just a legal piece of paper. Their relationship had never had an end, a finish line, answers, closure. He'd thought, if they tried sincerely talking to each other, that a mutual understanding might help them both get on with their lives.

Moonlight flooded through the windshield, making her skin look as soft and pale as vanilla. The ragged neck of her sweatshirt sagged low on her white throat. Strands of hair—golden, silky strands—swished around her cheeks when she laughed. She smelled like damask rose, and he remembered feeling like this before. He remembered sitting in a truck then, too, his father's, parked, somewhere, anywhere that they could be alone, just being with her enough to make the whole world go away, the hour getting late, knowing he had to take her home, never wanting to take her home.

When the pizza was gone, he scrunched up the box and napkins and tossed the debris in the back. Karen was still licking crumbs from her fingers, her lips still damp from her last sip of cola. Craig looked at her and knew damn well that his righteous motivations about "mutual understanding" and "closure" were worth horsefeathers.

He wanted to be with her. Like this. Alone. No matter what the cost, no matter what the risk.

"Reardon, I *have* to go in."

"I know."

"I doubt the girls even realize I'm gone, but you can't imagine what they can do to a house—"

"I know, I know."

She unfolded her legs and put a hand on the door lever, but she didn't open it. She hesitated, and then murmured, "It's a disgrace. A total disgrace—sneaking around at our age. Hiding out. Without question, this is the most illicit pizza I've had in years."

"You think that's why it tasted so good?"

"Could there be any doubt?" She chuckled, the dance of humor in her eyes, but then her tone softened. "Craig—thanks."

He told himself not to kiss her. He told himself that a good man would leave her alone, that Karen was wary of being hurt again, that he had too many guilty memories of getting her in trouble in the past.

Yet when he leaned closer, Kara made a disastrous mistake. She didn't pull away. When his palm cupped her face, she didn't move, didn't bolt. Her eyes shot to his, suddenly fever bright, wary and wanting both.

"Just one," he promised her.

"No."

"A kiss between friends."

"No."

"One. Very short, hands above the neck, may lightning strike me if it lasts longer than thirty seconds." A hundred years ago, he'd made the same bargain...and won the same nervous throaty chuckle.

"You were always a shameless hustler," she scolded.

"You loved being hustled, Kara." As soft as a whisper, his fingers slid into her hair. He could taste her sweet warm breath, she was so close. "By me. You loved being hustled by me, and you used to drive me crazy with your teasing. You'd get me so hot I couldn't see through the fog. Karen..." His tone changed, all humor gone. "It wasn't all hustling. When we were kids, I really believed I could slay all your dragons. I promised to keep you safe and take care of you, and I meant those promises. Maybe the only difference between then and now is that I'm older. Too old to make you promises that I can't guarantee."

She made a sound, a soft angry sound that came from the back of her throat, and he never had to take the kiss. She gave it. Her fingers dived in his hair and she covered his mouth in a deep kiss, a dark kiss, a kiss that sent a flush of fire through his whole body.

An untried girl asked for promises; a grown woman valued honesty. So she told him with a brazen trail of kisses down his jaw. She was sick of hurting, tired of living in that hell of past mistakes. So she told him with her hands, loosening from his hair only to flex and fold in tight fists around his neck.

She was scared out of her mind by what was happening between them.

So she told him by tracking kisses back to his mouth, by wetting his lips with the slow sweep of her tongue, by taking his mouth in a carnal kiss that the girl-Karen would never have dared.

She lifted her head. "I was never asking you for promises," she whispered fiercely. "I never expected them. If that's what you thought—"

"Shh," he murmured. The girl he'd fallen in love with had been a thousand times easier to handle. The woman in his arms was as volatile as a summer storm. Kara didn't know she was vulnerable. She was too busy being older, wiser, tougher.

"I'm not asking you for *anything*."

"I believe you. It's okay." He touched her cheek, wanting to soothe her, touch her, hold her. She was still trembling. Her eyes were a midnight blue and dark with desire, with want, with need, with all those promises she no longer believed in.

But a moment later she climbed out of the truck. He watched her weave through the shadows until she reached the front door and disappeared inside, and still he sat there.

The front seat of a Jeep Cherokee, in the middle of the night, was a heck of a time to discover that he was in love with his ex-wife. Not still in love, he mused broodingly, but falling deep, fast and painfully hard for the woman Karen had become. The woman he'd lost through carelessness and insensitivity. The one woman who might never believe another promise he made her, when finally Craig had a promise he could guarantee—that he'd changed.

To prove that to Karen, though, might just take dynamite.

Hytech was located a hop and skip from the grounds to the U.S. Air Force Academy. The company designed and manufactured fancy electronics for high-tech aircraft. No weapons, just gadgetry on a control panel for a pilot to play with.

The gadgetry, for reasons Craig had never fathomed, netted the company millions of dollars every year. Hytech liked that profit. They paid their marketing VP an annual six-figure income because they sincerely believed he was linked to that profit margin.

Some Mondays that was true. Not this one. Craig glanced at his watch for the third time in the past half hour, then gave marginal attention to the mess in front of him.

Papers were strewn the length of his office, blanketing the plush teal carpet. His two leather office chairs were pushed against the wall. Blueprints took up most of the space, with complex comparison studies of product performance lined up beneath them. A computer could have compared the products, but a computer never had and never would develop guts. Craig was paid for his gut instinct, and he had to physically see the whole picture before he could make a marketing decision on the potential product.

Virginia, his secretary, had locked the door to prevent a chance interruption, because the first puff of air would have sent the sea of papers in disarray. A pair of round-rimmed red glasses were perched on her ski jump of a nose. Her straight skirt was hiked to her knees, her ample fanny in the air as she shuffled through blueprints. Ginny had set up projects on his office carpet before. She should. She'd worked for him for the past ten years.

"We're never going to get this done if you keep looking at your watch, Reardon."

Craig pushed his shirtsleeve over the gold band. "I was just noticing that it was past four. You missed your break."

"I'll live. You're gonna be here all night if you don't have some help."

"So? That's not your problem."

"So you'd better take advantage of slave labor while you have it. I'm leaving at five. Dinner with Harv. Alone, no kids, no mother-in-law. So not even for you—much as I adore you—am I staying late tonight."

"Hey. Did I ask?"

"No." She pushed the oversize glasses higher on her nose. "But I hate to leave you alone with this. Not for your sake, for mine. If you work all night, you'll be crankier than an old bear tomorrow and even more aggravating to work with." She waited, expecting him to shoot back his own insult. He missed his cue. "You're ill," she said worriedly.

"Me? No, I'm fine."

"I don't think I've ever seen you this distracted."

"Just thinking," Craig said truthfully. Until that moment, he'd been thinking about a tiny keg of dynamite he'd set off in another office across town. Any minute now, he expected a phone call.

While he waited, though, he'd been thoughtfully evaluating his relationship with his assistant. When he first hired Virginia, she used to talk to him in awed, respectful tones. His godlike status hadn't lasted long. Ginny had seen him at his worst, and didn't give a cat's behind if he earned six figures or had a dozen titles on his door. She could be abrasive and outspoken, but she ran his office with ruthless efficiency and Craig knew damn well she loved her job.

It should have occurred to him before how similar Kara's job was. She, too, worked in an office for a company executive in an administrative role. In principle, Karen was a natural for business—she was a quick clear thinker, a whirlwind of energy, competent and cool in a crisis and terrific with people.

Because she never complained, Craig had always assumed that she liked her job. Now he was less than sure.

He vaguely recalled a time, two years ago, when Virginia had almost quit on him. Bracken, a smooth talker in accounting, had been sexually harassing her. When Craig found out, he'd had the jerk fired and read his assistant the riot act for not telling him what had been going on in the first place. Virginia, shook for once, said that these things happened in offices and she'd expected to handle it herself.

At some point over the years, as sure as the sun came up in the morning, an aggressive office Don Juan had come on to Karen. His Virginia was as plain as chicken soup. Karen was beautiful, hopelessly kind by nature and proud to a fault.

It was easy—so easy for him to see now—that she'd kept any hint of problems from him. Karen had brought home her raises, her successes, but never an upsetting story from the office or a clue if her job was less than satisfying.

And it had been nagging on him, all afternoon, that he'd never once roped her down and simply asked her if she had dreams, hopes, career goals in some other kind of work. How could he not know such an important thing about the woman he'd been married to?

The telephone jangled. He shot to his feet, earning him a startled look from Virginia. "I've been expecting a call. I'll take it in your office," he said swiftly.

He had to wade through the ocean of papers to even reach the door, but the side office was empty and private. He managed to grab the phone by the third ring. "Reardon here."

"Just who I wanted."

He snugged the receiver next to his ear, feeling a grin already tugging the corners of his mouth. Reality was even better than anticipation. The feminine voice on the other end was a familiar husky alto—and full of pique.

"A florist delivered flowers to my desk this afternoon," she informed him.

"Yeah?" He forgot Virginia, his office, his work, and mentally pictured Karen. She was fussy about how she dressed for work. She'd have her hair swept up. She'd be wearing killer heels, because Kara was a sucker for killer heels, and she'd have on one of those no-nonsense business suits. She'd look sharp. She'd look competently, efficiently, undestroyably put together. It would take a teensy stick of dynamite to put that rattled wobble in her voice.

"They were roses. Three dozen roses. Three dozen *yellow* roses. The card was signed 'Tex Lancer.'"

"Sounds like this Tex is a real admirer of yours," Craig commented.

"And cows fly. I don't know any Tex Lancer."

"You sure? Maybe you met him somewhere and just don't remember."

"*Reardon.* There's only one person who would send me yellow tea roses and it isn't anybody named Tex. How could you do this to me?"

"Me? Honey, you're blaming the wrong guy. It's not my fault that you have men chasing after you."

"Craig—"

"Damn. The other line's ringing. I can't talk now, Kara, but I'll catch you a little later."

She was still sputtering when he hung up. Craig chuckled aloud, thinking wickedly that his ex-wife had a long week of sputtering ahead of her.

The florist order he'd placed that morning only began with the roses. Tomorrow, Kara was going to get an armload of camellias from Clifford Raines. Wednesday, Basil Wickenford III was going to send her orchids. Thursday, violets from Gilbert Rafferty. On Friday, Quentin Forbes...what the devil had Quentin Forbes sent her? Those long stalky things with lots of flashy color. The florist had described them, but Craig wasn't very good at remembering the names of flowers.

Apparently he'd been just as bad at making her feel appreciated a long time ago.

Trust lost was as irretrievable as secrets told. And Craig knew it would take heavier artillery than some handfuls of flowers to win and woo Kara. She didn't want to be wooed. She didn't want to be hurt again, and her wariness was well-founded. She'd been married to a selfish, insensitive jerk.

The mistakes he'd made weighed like grief on his heart, but they were done. Unerasable. Indelibly part of their past. His only hope was to prove to Kara that he was a different man, prove, incontestably, that he wouldn't hurt her again.

This time, Craig resolved, he would be infinitely careful with Kara. This time he'd make damn sure he caused her no trouble. This time, he'd make it right for her.

Six

Karen was sorting clothes in the utility room when she heard the rap on the back door. "Julie? Can you answer it? I'm really over my head in here."

"Sure."

Karen heard the broom drop in the kitchen. Julie was thrilled for any interruption of Saturday-morning chores, and she wasn't the lone stranger. Blowing a strand of hair from her eyes, Karen bent over the clothes pile. It was her considered opinion that all clothing manufacturers had a sadistic streak. Every shirt, every blouse, every pair of pants came with a different set of washing instructions. Three people, ninety-seven weekly wash loads. Was this nuts or what?

"Well, hi, Dad!"

Karen abruptly straightened. She could hear the surprise in her daughter's voice even through a mouthful of donut.

"I thought we weren't going riding until this afternoon."

Craig swung an arm around his daughter and bussed her cheek. "We're not."

"You need me?"

"Not exactly."

"You need Jon, then. Man, will he be glad. He's upstairs in the war zone—and that's no exaggeration, the state of his room. You can't imagine—"

"I don't exactly need Jon, either. I need your mother."

Julie hesitated. "Mom?" Her eyes widened. "You need Mom?"

"Actually, what I need are some old tax forms. She used to keep them up in the attic. At least I'm hoping she'll know where they are. Is she home?"

"Yes, she's home," Karen said from the doorway. Conscious of the interest and curiosity in their daughter's eyes, she greeted Craig with a polite nod. Her pulse, though, was fluttering like frantic bird wings.

All week her ex-husband had been as impossible to catch as a thief. She'd reached him the one time about the roses, but that was it. Suddenly he was remarkably tied up in meetings when she'd tried to call at work, and amazingly too busy to answer his telephone at home.

All those incredible, unforgettable flowers.... Craig was in terrible trouble with her. At just that instant, he didn't seem to realize it. He was wearing old button-fly jeans and a zipped-up leather jacket, his hands in his pockets and his face ruddy from the sting-cold morning outside. Typical of her ex-husband's behavior, he stood in the doorway with a leg cocked forward, not venturing a step farther without her permission. Also typical of her ex-husband's behavior, his gaze took in her appearance—her snug slim jeans and rolled-up red-sleeved shirt—with a blank expression. The dark eyes meeting hers were unfailingly remote, his voice unbudgeably civil.

"I'm sorry to bother you, Karen, but if you have a minute... I'm almost sure there are some old accounting records in the attic. If you wouldn't mind my taking a look, I'd appreciate it."

"It's no problem," she said politely. "You need—"

"The tax returns for 1987."

"Ah." She shrugged ruefully. "I'm afraid they're buried pretty deep. Julie—"

Her daughter hastily held up her hands. "Count me out. I don't know where anything is up there."

"Well, I'll go up with you, then." With her spine as stiff as a poker, Karen led the way up the stairs, past the three bedrooms and bath. Craig never said another word until Jon poked his head out the door.

"Dad! What on earth are you—"

"We're just trying to track down some old accounting records," Craig told him.

"We think they're in the attic," Karen told him. At the end of the hall, she turned the handle on the small arched door that led to the attic. Craig paused to exchange a few more words with Jon Jacob, but she went on ahead.

The stairs were narrow, steep and dark. Once up, light filtered through two half-moon windows at each end. The attic had never been finished. Wind whipped through the cracks, and dusty sunlight illuminated the barren plank floor, raw slanting beams and the boxes and piles of debris.

Wrapping her arms under her chest, Karen whisked a glance over the mess—high chairs and cribs, a broken rocker, an old turntable, endless boxes of books. The attic stored a hundred memories, but no tax returns. The attic had never been used to store tax returns—his, hers or anyone else's.

Which Craig knew.

She heard him latch the door below, then bound up the creaking steps. He never stopped at the top but kept coming, straight toward her. His gaze was no longer remote. His expression no longer looked civil, or even kin to civilized.

He strode toward her like a pirate for fresh-found loot, angled his head and stole a kiss. Technically the kiss was short enough to pass for a greeting. It was still long enough for her to feel the crush of cold leather against her breasts, catch the scent of wind on his skin, inhale the tease of his soft mouth on hers. Her lungs shuttled in oxygen when he raised his head—with a grin full of hell.

"Good morning, Kara," he murmured, as innocent as a Boy Scout.

Lord, he was bad. Her heart was thundering like a pagan drumroll, which Karen told herself was disgraceful. Fooling the children, sneaking around, secret meetings . . . of course, there was no other choice,

not if they were to protect the kids from building unrealistic expectations. But it still felt wicked.

Deliciously wicked. For the past year, she'd lived as
chastely as a nun. She'd almost forgotten the dangerously alluring taste of doing something just a little
bad, a little forbidden. And there was only one unconscionable rogue who'd ever teased her with that
kind of temptation. The one, now, who squeezed her
shoulders as if they were easy old pals and swept past
her.

"Craig—" There was an important reason she
needed to talk to him. Any second now, she was going to remember it.

Her ex-husband clearly had his own agenda. "I figured, at most, we could steal twenty minutes." Craig
hooked a leg over a box of books and motioned her
closer. "I brought you something. That's why I came
over. But first, coffee." He unzipped his leather jacket
and brought out a narrow silver thermos like a tro-
phy. "Only one cup. We'll have to share. And then an
itsy-bitsy present—"

"A present? No. Craig, just wait a minute—"

"Don't get nervous. I promise, it's no big thing."

He plopped a square wrapped package in her lap
almost before she could sink down on the wooden
crate next to him. Her eyes were on his face, not the
package.

"Come on, come on, open it. If you don't, I will."

Impatiently he watched her peel off the yellow
wrapping paper. Beneath the paper was a book. She'd
barely mentioned, and only once, the class she'd taken
in Chinese history. The book was on the history of

Chinese art, a classic edition, trimmed in gold leaf and beautifully bound in saddle leather.

Craig looked alarmed at the expression on her face. "I thought you'd like it."

"I do."

"I thought it would go along. With the history you were interested in. But, hell, Kara, I don't know anything about the subject—"

"It's perfect. An absolutely wonderful gift. A treasure." Her voice came out thick, as if she'd been licking honey off a spoon. Deliberately she cleared her throat. "This is dirty pool, Reardon—and you know it."

"Dirty pool?"

"You said we'd go slow. You said we'd just see. You can't do things like this. It isn't right, it isn't fair, and it's totally confusing me—"

"Yeah?" He sounded pleased that she was confused. Arrogantly pleased, like a man holding a jack and an ace, who'd never gambled before.

"Craig...it's no good," she said firmly.

"What's no good?"

"If the reason for the book and all those flowers was to make things up to me. It's no good." Now she remembered the talk she'd been fueling up for all week. "I thought a lot about what you said. About feeling guilty for getting me in trouble. But you have it all wrong. You never had anything to make up. You never talked me into sleeping with you—I wanted to. You never talked me into eloping—I wanted to. You were never, ever responsible for pushing me into anything."

"Okay."

She shook her head. "No, it's *not* okay. If I'd known you were carrying that guilt load around, I'd have strangled you. Heaven knows we were both damn fools, but I get full credit for being half of that damnfool team. You don't get any extra blame. You don't get any extra hair shirts. Any trouble we got into, every single time, we were equally responsible for. Have you got that straight?"

"Kara?"

"Hmm?" All along, she thought distractedly, she should have helped him with that guilt business. Craig's parents were good to the kids and Karen got on with them fine, but years ago the Reardons had lived in the fast lane and divorced over one of their idiotic "open relationships." Even back in school Craig never talked about it, but she thought his overdeveloped sense of guilt started with them. He'd cultivated a wild reputation that was no more than flash and show. At heart he craved stability and commitment, and always—always—had been relentlessly hard on himself.

Craig's knuckles curled under her chin, diverting her attention away from that thought train. It just wasn't a moment to dissect the past. She had a man who was definitely trying to claim her attention in the present.

"Don't frown," he ordered her.

Because the command was so silly, she stopped frowning.

"I didn't give you the book out of guilt, sunshine."

"No?" The brush of his knuckles was evocative, teasing, but there was an oddly intense glint in his eyes.

"No. The gift was a whim, nothing more. And I'll be damned if I know why Tex sent you those roses, but it's my masculine intuition that his motivation had nothing to do with guilt, either."

It was a nonsense conversation since there was obviously no Tex, but Karen fed along. "So...what does your masculine intuition tell you was the reason for Tex—and his sidekicks—sending me those flowers?"

"The obvious." Craig dropped his hand and was suddenly busy, unscrewing the thermos and pouring a lid of coffee. "You're a beautiful, talented, sexy woman, Kara. A rare combination, which a man would have to be deaf, dumb and blind not to appreciate. I'm not surprised there are men giving you a rush—but that doesn't mean I want to hear the details. In fact, I'd just as soon not hear any more about those flowers."

His tone was gruff, and he was so busy with that lid of coffee that he couldn't meet her eyes. The compliment touched her, but not half as much as watching him fiddling, fiddling, fiddling with that damn lid. His shoulders were big as a house and his hands deliberately steady...yet she'd never, Karen thought, seen him more vulnerable.

Until that moment, she hadn't known that he was playing for keeps. He had definitely heard her, about feeling unappreciated and taken for granted. Just as she'd heard him—about feeling responsible for the mistakes they'd made.

They were listening to each other. She'd never thought it would happen again. And her heart suddenly felt the assault of something dangerously, perilously, terrifyingly...soft.

"Okay," she murmured lightly. "If you don't want to hear any more about the flowers, I won't say another word."

"Good," he said.

"But I have to tell you that it bothers me to leave it like this. If I only knew the real identity of who'd given me those flowers, I was going to strip stark naked, dress up in a veil or two and seduce him to the rhythm of *Bolero* by way of a thank-you."

Craig choked on his coffee. She politely handed him a napkin, which he ignored. His eyes shot to her face, with a pinning gaze that made her heartbeat slam. "Maybe we'll see if Tex can manage to list a return address next time."

"You think Tex would appreciate a personal thank-you?"

"I think, without any effort at all, you could drive Tex clear out of his mind."

"Well, I wouldn't want to go that far," Karen murmured. "But if you think he wouldn't like the *Bolero* idea, I had a second thought involving firelight and maraschino cherries and a little champagne."

"Karen?"

"Hmm?"

"If you keep this up, I might be tempted to forget there are two impressionable teenagers below and start chasing you around this attic." He was teasing, then again, he wasn't. The dusty light fell on his stark, strong profile. For a moment he didn't move, didn't even seem to be breathing. "I thought you were scared, honey."

PLAY THE
CARNIVAL WHEEL

scratch-off game
and get as many as
SIX FREE GIFTS . . .

HOW TO PLAY

1. With a coin, carefully scratch off the silver area at right. Then check your number against the chart below it to find out which gifts you're eligible to receive.

2. You'll receive brand-new Silhouette Desire® novels and possibly other gifts—ABSOLUTELY FREE! Send back this card and we'll promptly send you the free books and gift(s) you qualify for!

3. We're betting you'll want more of these heart-warming romances, so unless you tell us otherwise, every month we'll send you 6 more wonderful novels to read and enjoy. Always delivered right to your home months before they arrive in stores. And always at a discount off the cover price!

4. Your satisfaction is guaranteed! You may return any shipment of books and cancel at any time. The Free Books and Gift(s) remain yours to keep!

NO COST! NO RISK!
NO OBLIGATION TO BUY!

More Good News For Subscribers-Only!

When you join the Silhouette Reader Service™, you'll receive 6 heart-warming romance novels each month delivered to your home. You'll also get additional free gifts from time to time as well as our subscribers-only newsletter. It's your privileged look at upcoming books and profiles of our most popular authors!

If offer card is missing, write to:
Silhouette Reader Service, 3010 Walden Avenue, P.O. Box 1867, Buffalo, NY 14269-1867

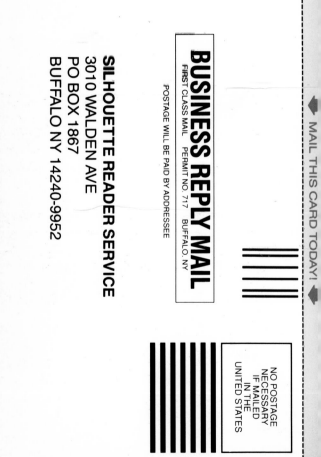

MAIL THIS CARD TODAY!

BUSINESS REPLY MAIL

FIRST CLASS MAIL   PERMIT NO. 717   BUFFALO, NY

POSTAGE WILL BE PAID BY ADDRESSEE

SILHOUETTE READER SERVICE
3010 WALDEN AVE
PO BOX 1867
BUFFALO NY 14240-9952

NO POSTAGE
NECESSARY
IF MAILED
IN THE
UNITED STATES

"I was. I am." She took a breath. "But it's not going to work if either of us holds back, is it? Either we're honest or we're not. Either we both give it one hundred percent of another try... or there's no point in trying at all." Her lips curved in a shaky smile. "I'm not sure a bookie would take odds on us making it, Reardon."

He reached out to tuck a tendril of hair behind her ear. His touch lingered. "To hell with the bookies. This is how we discovered each other the first time— just the two of us, alone, one-on-one. And this time we'll be more careful, Kara."

Karen saw the way he looked at her, felt the way he touched her and knew darn well that being careful was the last thing on her ex-husband's mind. There was enough darn heat in his eyes to make her nerves feel buttered and toasted. She unfolded her legs and sprang to her feet. "We've been here too long. The kids will be wondering. I'd better go down."

"Hey. You're gonna leave me up here, trying to find a tax form that doesn't exist?"

"Yup."

"Come back here, sunshine."

She continued—judiciously—jogging for the stairwell. Craig was only going to kiss her if she stayed. She sincerely doubted that he would settle for one lonesome kiss. It would be easy, as easy as madness, to let a couple of kisses explode into trouble.

She had a history of losing her head with him. She needed to remember that. Neither of them had ever done anything slower than at breakneck speeds—especially in the area of chemistry and sex. She needed to remember that, too.

Maybe she loved him. Maybe she'd never stopped loving him. Maybe, just maybe, she'd swim through a flood if she thought they could make it this time. But other people, especially the children, had been affected by their mistakes before. Hurt had taught her caution; experience had forced her to develop responsible judgment.

She'd made it down three steps before Craig's head popped over the wooden railing. The devil was wearing a grin that no decent woman would trust.

"If you're gonna desert me," he scolded, "the least you can do is tell me what you had in mind for those cherries."

From the look in his eyes, he was envisioning her lapping up a maraschino cherry from his bare navel.

Abruptly, so was she.

She raised her eyes to the rafters. "What am I going to do with you, Reardon?" she muttered.

"You really want me to answer that?"

"No."

She shut the door on him, still in the attic, before releasing a bubbling, throaty chuckle. Threatened with a tornado, stranded on the high seas without a raft, buried in an avalanche in the Rockies . . . Craig would still be fun.

It was one of the things she'd always loved about him.

It was one of the things that warned her how deep and how fast she was already over her head.

Jon considered his sister a cross between the bubonic plague and a complete pain. From the day she was born, she'd been tagging after him. Everybody was always proud of her because she brought home all *A*'s from school. She was nosy and sneaky and she messed with his stuff. It was understood—by Dad, anyway—that he'd watch out for her at school, which was no small job since she got boobs. Twice he'd come home from fights, both with senior guys, both jocks, who were under the mistaken impression that his sister was fair game. He hated fights. How come he got stuck with a sister who was a looker?

She was the bane of his life, but there was one good thing he had to say about Jule. She didn't tell. Backed to a wall, threatened with being grounded for life, she still never told. In times of trouble they stuck together. He came through for her; she came through for him. The system worked reliably well in dealing with parents.

Usually.

Peering out the kitchen window, Julie watched the car drive away. "Where'd Mom say she was going?"

"To get milk."

His sister promptly crossed the room and pulled open the refrigerator door. "Look." He looked, over her shoulder, at the five quarts of milk sitting neatly on the shelves. They exchanged glances. "This is the third time this week, and I don't get it. Where is she *going?*"

"Pretty obviously to get milk," Jon said dryly.

"I *know* that. Cripes, if she brings home any more milk, we might as well start a dairy. And did you see how she was dressed? White wool slacks and a burgundy sweater?" Jon looked blank. The significance of the clothes went right over his head. "*Jon.* Since when does Mom dress to go to a quick stop? She's obviously just bringing home milk to cover her tracks.''

Jon grabbed a quart just before she closed the door, and took a long gulp from the carton. "She'll be back by eight. The other times, she was never gone more than an hour. Maybe she's just shopping."

"And cats swim." Julie sank in a chair, her chin in her hands. "Now it's seven o'clock at night and we don't know where our own mother is, and I think you should do something."

"Me? What am I supposed to do?" Jon wiped his mouth on the back of his sleeve.

"At *least* admit you're worried."

"Okay. I admit it. She's been acting weird, but so, big deal, maybe she's doing something that she doesn't want us to know about."

"God, you're dense," Julie said wearily. "Of *course,* she's doing something that she doesn't want us to know about. Why do you think I'm worried, dummkopf? Mom's never kept a secret from us. We're her whole life."

Jon didn't deny that, but offered, "I think it's Dad."

"You wanna believe it's Dad. I wanna believe it's Dad. But what if it isn't? What if it's some other guy? Or what if she's in some kind of trouble and really *needs* us?"

Jon took another swig of milk. It stuck in his throat like a cold lump. Par for the course, his sister was being overdramatic and annoying. What she said still bothered him, though. "Maybe you're right," he said slowly, "but I don't want to catch any more hell for interfering."

"Who's talking about interfering? I'm just talking about watching out for her. Making sure she's okay. *Helping* her."

There was no way Jon couldn't agree with that.

A week before, Karen had worried that the chemistry between them was building out of control. Every time they were together, desire sprung up like an unruly wind. A look, a touch, and the air between them increasingly charged with expectation, anticipation. Passion wasn't new. But they were. As a couple, as a man and woman, Karen knew there was nothing the same. Her pull toward Craig eclipsed anything she'd felt before. It also made her afraid.

A foolish fear, she'd discovered.

The sexual intimacy she was afraid would happen too fast...there'd been zip, zero and none. Heaven knew how illicit lovers managed to conduct an affair. She and Craig had to conspire like thieves to steal an hour at a time together.

Streetlights danced by, dazzling prisms in the rain. The evening was pitch-dark, and rain sluiced down her windshield in cold silver rivulets. She leaned forward to increase the speed on the wipers.

"You sure you want to drive?" Craig asked her. "It's coming down pretty hard."

"I'm fine. And we're not going that far."

"You're still not going to tell our mysterious destination?"

She glanced at him with a rueful smile. "It's away from the madding crowd. I promise you that."

Truthfully she was a little uneasy at the choice of place she was taking him, but needs must where the devil drove. She wanted—*needed*—time alone with Craig. How could she know her feelings, or his, without a chance to test and explore them? Yet she'd been cautious, and responsible enough, to suggest meetings on neutral ground—nice, safe, innocuous places where desire had no chance to eclipse their better sense. Further, no one familiar was likely to run into them at the library. Or the art museum. Or the little out-of-the-way deli on Colfax Street.

Karen peeled down her window an inch. It let in rain, but the defroster simply couldn't keep up with the humid fog.

They'd been "safe" nowhere. Forget sex. The problem had been exposure, and the humorous—or not so humorous—angle of that problem had been ducking and dodging their own kids. There was no specific reason why Jon Jacob shouldn't be buying a corned beef on rye in the deli, or for that matter, why he might not take a girl on a cheap date at the museum. And Julie often used the library, but rarely, in Karen's memory, during the evening hours.

Traveling a distance would have guaranteed them a private place to talk. Only neither of them had mountains of spare time to waste on travel and distance, and neither had anticipated that the innocent desire to talk with each other would prove such a problem.

Karen adored the children. So did Craig. If push came to shove, she'd have killed for her children. So would Craig. But tonight Jon Jacob had a date and was using Craig's Cherokee. Julie was sleeping overnight at a friend's. The chance of a few solid hours together had been unexpected, and Karen was determined to take advantage of them.

"I seem to remember this turn," Craig murmured.

He should, she thought.

"Ah, sunshine? You wouldn't be thinking of doing anything illegal, now would you?"

"I'm thirty-six years old, trying hard to be a good role model for our mutual children and have held down a responsible job for years. Does that sound like a woman who'd even *think* of doing something illegal?"

The blacktop was as shiny as wet ebony in the rain. She glanced ahead, then in the rearview mirror. No other car was in sight. She turned the wheel off the smooth road and directly onto rough terrain.

One of Colorado Springs' special spots was the Garden of the Gods, a thirteen-hundred-acre park that the native Indians used to call "the Redlands." It was a place where prairie met mountain, where erosion had formed mystically sculpted rocks, where granite had been weathered, frozen and thawed for centuries. Red rock climbed to form cathedral spires. Juniper trees twisted in impossibly gnarled shapes. Nature had created a wonder, a surprise, behind every turn.

The park was closed at night and had always been. The boundaries of the park, though, were not exactly as secure as Fort Knox. She and Craig had found a way in when they were kids—first drawn because it was forbidden, which made it fun, and then drawn, time after time, because it was a special spot where they could be guaranteed alone.

Karen killed the engine and pushed the button on the headlights. For a few moments, the inside of the car was blacker than pitch. Her passenger had turned in the seat, but he hadn't said a word. The only sound was the rain . . . and the erratic cadence of her heart.

"I couldn't think of any other place," she said helplessly. "The kids came close to finding us everywhere we tried to go. We've been ducking out back doors like criminals. If it wasn't the kids, it could just as well have been someone else. Too darn many people know us. And this was the only place I could think of where no one could conceivably guess where we'd be."

If a fox could talk on entering a henhouse, it would have Craig's wicked voice. "You don't have to come up with excuses, Kara. I understand. You brought me here to neck."

"No—"

"You're hot for my bod. Admit. I mean, come on— that was *my* excuse when we were seventeen, that I was only bringing you up here to have a place to 'talk.' You think I'm naive?"

"Reardon . . ." Slowly the tension eased out of her shoulders and she started to chuckle. It was exactly what she'd been afraid of—that he'd jump to the wrong conclusions if she brought him here—and Craig obviously remembered their less-than-chaste history in this spot. A dozen first times had happened here. The first time he'd used his tongue in a kiss. The first time she'd used hers. The first time she'd let him near bare skin, the first time she'd felt the heady ache and song of real desire, the first time he'd coaxed her hand to discover that strangely threatening bulge beneath his zipper.

So many years had passed that Karen assumed the ghost of those old memories would have faded. They had. Until she stopped the car. And felt the blood rush straight to her head with anxiety and nerves.

That moment was gone—or fast disappearing. How could she hold on to a terrible case of nerves? Her ex-partner in all those memories was loving the whole situation, hamming it up with a waggling pair of eyebrows and a campy vampire leer.

"Hell, honey. If you don't keep your hands off me, I'll try to bear up." His dramatic sigh belonged on a stage. "A man has to do what a man has to do."

"Stop, you egotistical maniac."

"Now, Kara. Really, it's all right. I'm willing to sacrifice my virtue, but only for you. I wouldn't want it spread around that I parked with any girl who asked me...." A hesitation, then a grave observation. "You're choking, honey. I'll help all I can. Really. But I have to confess it's gonna be tricky for me to get in the mood if you keep laughing."

Seven

His outrageous teasing finally made her laugh. And when she laughed, she relaxed. Karen had obviously worried what he'd think about coming back here.

Craig wisely didn't tell her. On first sight of the place, he'd felt a slam in the pit of his belly. Old memories seemed cocooned in the car: the beat of darkness, of secrets whispered, of emotions freed when they were alone together. It was in this place that they'd both discovered the power of sexual feelings, but they'd found also another kind of intimacy. Kara was a mystery where he had to coax for a clue; she'd never easily talked about herself. Yet here, in this place, she'd opened up for him.

Craig thought—*hoped* he could make that happen again.

"Look," she said.

Rain poured down from a mercury-colored sky. Lightning crackled on the far horizon, bathing the landscape with an eerie silver. For an instant, the park transformed into a fairyland. The tall spires of rock looked like the turrets of a huge castle, with diamonds for windows and jewels in every shadow.

Karen leaned forward to rub the fog from the windshield. "There's nothing out there but rock and sand," she murmured. "But in a storm, or under moonlight, it's like no other place on earth. The stuff of imagination and dreams."

"You always loved this place."

"Because it's impossibly beautiful."

So, Craig thought, was she. Rain shimmied down the car windows, reflecting light and shadow on her delicate features. Kara never thought of herself as a sensual woman. He'd never thought of her any other way. Her skin was as soft as a brush of honey, her eyes luminous in the semidarkness. She'd left her hair loose, brushed back from her brow, and it was mussed now in a sleepy tangle of silver and gold.

She'd called, then picked him up, five minutes after the kids' plans had gelled. The spur-of-the-moment outing had given her no time to fuss with clothes or makeup. Beneath a hastily pulled-on light jacket, she wore a denim skirt and a fuzzy coral sweater that buttoned to the throat. The jacket wasn't warm enough, the skirt impractical for the chill-cold dampness of the night.

Again she pressed against the steering wheel to rub a circle on the windshield. "Quit breathing, Reardon. I can't see out."

He grinned. "It's just my breathing that's the problem, is it? *Don't* crack the window—you're already freezing."

"I'm not. I'm warm as toast."

She opened the window an inch and then swiveled toward him, offering him an easy opportunity to confiscate a slim white hand. Her fingers were icebergs.

Caught in the fib, she grumbled plaintively. "Well, who could have guessed it would be this cold in September?"

"Anyone who lived in Colorado," he teased her. At this time of year, the weather changed quickly and unpredictably. Already there was snow on the mountain peaks, where spare weeks ago they'd made love on a sultry warm day in the cabin.

He remembered that day with every intimate detail in vivid color. So, he suspected, did Kara.

When he didn't release her hand, her gaze shot to his, midnight soft and wary with sudden, sharp sexual tension. Yet all he did, patiently, was fit her freezing hands into his worn sheepskin gloves. On her they looked bigger than boxer's mitts, making her chuckle, although her eyes still lingered on his.

The storm was building on its race west. Yet another set of lightning bolts lit up the far horizon. The view distracted her attention yet again.

"More stuff of dreams?" he murmured.

She turned her head. "Don't you feel it, too?"

He could feel the rare vulnerability of her mood. All that mattered. "What if you could make a dream real, sunshine? Imagine, just for fun, if you could go anywhere, do something you'd always really wanted to do...."

She closed her eyes, liking the game. "If I could travel anywhere, hands down—I'd head for the Far East. Especially China. And I suppose if I could do something I really wanted..." She promptly opened her eyes, tensed up. "You'll laugh."

"I won't."

"It's just a stupid dream. Nothing big or sweeping. Nothing even particularly interesting—"

"Tell me."

She hesitated. "When we were in high school, I didn't know anyone—any girl—who wanted to teach. For a career, teaching was just too much of an old-fashioned female stereotype. But I always wanted to do something with kids and history. It's just..." She lifted a hand. "I've watched our own kids. They think history is nothing more than memorizing some dry old dates—nothing that really affects them. But it *should* affect them, if it's taught right. A lot of history is a record of mistakes we don't want to make again. And kids need to know there's a huge world out there, other places, other values and cultures, other people with our same problems and different ideas about those problems...." She stopped dead, as if mortified to discover she'd been bubbling on like a fast-running brook.

"Go on," he urged her.

"I *like* children," she said defensively.

As if this were a shocking fact to him. In a room with a hundred people and a toddler, Karen would instinctively gravitate toward the toddler. At an age when most parents cringed at a gathering of teenagers, her door was always wide open. Kara, as long as he'd known her, had always drawn kids like a pied piper.

"It's just an old pipe dream," she assured him with a little laugh. "Something I used to think about. A long time ago."

He couldn't stop looking at her face. "Nothing that matters to you anymore, hmm?"

"Heavens, no. Good grief, I have a good-paying job with security and a future. What kind of impression would it make on the kids if I just irresponsibly threw that all away—and for absolutely nothing sure. Ah, Craig?"

"I'm listening. But you're starting to shiver." The problem of cold could have been resolved by turning on the car engine and heater. Instead, he pushed up the console between the seats and reached for her, which solved a more critical problem. Getting her close. Now. Kara didn't immediately object to being hauled on his lap—but then she was cold. And he was still talking. "You'd never consider going back to school?"

"To take a course now and then, sure. But to finish a degree—"

He filled in the blank. "There's no possible spare time."

"Exactly. I work eight to five. There's the house to take care of. And much more important—"

"Much more important, the kids need you."

"Yes."

"And you do a lot for your parents. Your mother depends on you, especially since your sisters moved out of state. When it all adds up, you barely have a free minute now, much less time to go back to school again.''

''None. And I'm not sure why we're still talking about this. We were just talking idle dreams, remember? The idea was pure foolishness.'' She added humorously, ''And so is this, Reardon.''

''I'm just trying to get you warm.'' He'd opened his jacket and snuggled her closer.

''Why don't I trust your altruistic motives?''

''Because you're irrationally suspicious?'' He nuzzled the crown of her head with his cheek. Her eyes had been full of fire when she'd talked about kids and teaching. It made him ache, wondering how long she'd suppressed that dream. It made him aware how often, with him, with the kids, with her family, Karen had put everyone else's needs ahead of her own. ''You have nothing to worry about. I'll take care of everything.''

''Somehow that statement fails to inspire trust when your hand is sneaking under my jacket.''

''Nothing interesting is going to happen. An acrobat couldn't make anything interesting happen in the front seat of a car, much less in these temperatures. However...''

She angled her head to look at him. Her eyes were lush with laughter, her lips tipped in a beguiling curve. ''However?'' she prompted him.

''However, it occurred to me that we should do a performance study on whether necking techniques have changed in the past fifteen years. An intellectual performance study. For posterity.''

''That's a pitiful line, Reardon.''

He knew, but Kara didn't seem to mind. There was just a hint of recklessness in her languid smile. She had no fear of necking, because no spark could light a forest fire, not here, not now. She was sure of that. Very sure.

Craig coaxed her to feel even more secure. He never touched her sweater except to roll down the high collar. The angora fabric tickled his chin when he laid his lips on her throat. Her skin was soft and white and smelled like Shalimar. He knew the scent. Maybe she didn't remember, but certain nights, under the sheets, he'd discovered that fragrance in some unexpected places.

Heat flamed low in his groin, yet he mapped a safe, slow trail of kisses from her throat to the shell of her ear. His tongue collided with a pearl-drop earring. She murmured something teasing. He reached up, and with a finger pushed at the post until both parts of the earring dropped in his palm.

She fell silent. And that hint of recklessness in her smile suddenly disappeared.

He ambushed the shell of her ear again, this time free to nibble on the unprotected lobe. A sigh whooshed out of her lungs. He found her mouth, and slowly, persuasively wet her lips with his tongue. He kissed her again, deeper this time, exploring the honeyed warmth of her mouth with slow greed and intimate thoroughness. He heard a plop. Then another plop as she peeled off his gloves and hurled them in the back seat.

She didn't touch him, but her gaze mirrored the desire to—and fear of that desire. Her eyes were dilated, one click out of focus, fuzzy and vulnerable. She wasn't sure of him. Not anymore.

"Do it," he said. "Touch me. I want to feel your hands on me."

She tried her best excuse. "They're still cold. You'll die."

"I won't die. Do it, Kara."

Under the blanket of jackets, she slipped her hands under his sweater. She'd warned him, yet his breath still caught for the first feel of her chilled fingertips. Her hands thawed, then warmed, then heated on the bare skin of his abdomen. Desire ripped through him, sharper than a knife blade.

He'd missed her touch. Like a chip from his soul, he'd missed her touch. Her hair shimmered through his fingers like silvery silk when he angled her chin for another kiss. With her hands trapped under his sweater, he stroked the length of her until he found the edge of her skirt.

The rain poured down in torrents, but in the car it was quiet. So quiet that he could hear her breath hoarsen, weaken. So quiet that he could hear the whisper of his palm stroking, gliding the length of her silk stockings from ankle to calf to knee. Then higher up her thigh.

She twisted, making a rough-sweet sound against his lips. His lover, always, had been slow to waken...and then impossible to put back to sleep. Kara...was restless. Impatient. Aroused. In the dark-fogged car, under a tangled confusion of coats and clothes, he kneaded the firm supple skin of her thigh. She let that happen. But when he dipped his fingers in the crevice between her legs, her muscles clamped hard on his wrist. She whispered, "Craig...no."

"Shh." He kissed her again. "All your clothes are on. Nothing's going to happen that you need to worry about. Trust me."

He took her mouth in a tumble of deepening, darkening kisses. Below, through her hose, he found the patch of warmth and silky dampness he sought. At that instant, there was no goal in his head beyond touching her and sharing an intimate moment of pleasure. But that goal changed when her pulse quickened and her breathing turned shallow and erratic. Kara never expected to be taken under.

Neither did he. Thunder growled in the distance, reflecting the storm of frustration infecting his whole body. There was birth control in his pocket, which he had no prayer of using, not here, not now, not under these circumstances. His right foot was falling asleep, his shoulder cramping, and the last place he wanted to be was in a car. He wanted a mattress. With Kara stark naked. Behind a locked door.

And still his palm cupped and rubbed and stroked through the barrier of hose, hating the barrier of hose, thinking that this was all her fault. He'd never planned this. All he'd planned, this night, was coaxing her to talk. But then she had, about that dream, and all he could think about were all the dreams she'd put aside over the years, for the kids, for him. Kara had always made it easy for him to be selfish.

So it was her own damn fault she was in trouble now. She tried to twist around him, and couldn't. She tried to free her hands, and couldn't. "Reardon," she breathed.

"Let me." Scent shimmered off her skin as her temperature climbed. He tuned out his own needs, tuned in only to her and what he wanted her to feel. "Let me, Kara...." Fever glistened in her eyes, fueled by desire and frustration and a vulnerability that was hard, so hard, for her to risk. Yet she'd trusted him once.

He kissed her nose, her cheek, then sealed her mouth in a kiss of poured emotion. He wasn't the same, selfish boy. He needed her to know that, believe it. It seemed a simple gift he wanted to offer, yet the emotions reflected on her face weren't at all simple. Her neck arched. His lips laid on the pulse beat of her throat when her legs suddenly trapped his hand, coiling tight with friction and pressure. She cried out, a fierce sharp whisper, as her body contracted for a first spasm of pleasure, and then a rush that turned her eyes liquid.

For a long time after that, he didn't move. A brief flash of yellow lights registered in his peripheral vision, but only vaguely. He was just as vaguely aware that there was perspiration on his forehead, that he was hard to the point of torture and that all circulation had been cut off from his left leg.

And then Kara tilted back her head, and the rest didn't matter. Tenderness nearly engulfed him. Bangs clung damply to her brow. Her fingertips touched his cheek with softness and wonder. She still wasn't breathing well. And her eyes. God, her eyes. He never thought she'd look at him like that again.

"I'm so mad at you—" her thumb streaked across his cheekbone "—that I can hardly talk."

"Yeah?" Gently, unwillingly, he withdrew his hand and rearranged her clothes. Maybe, by next year, he could find the strength to take his eyes off her. Her mouth was bruised red and damp, a trembling rose petal suffering from the same wild wind that had tangled her hair. She looked as if she wanted to stretch like a languid sleepy cat, but he hoped she didn't. If she moved at all, she was likely to cause him bodily harm.

"This was all your fault," she accused him.

"I sure hope so."

"Stop smiling at me. I'm embarrassed to death. That wasn't *necking*, Reardon, and I can't believe you did this to me in a car." Sensual humor twinkled in her eyes, and something more. She ran the tip of her fingers across his bottom lip. "You're dangerous, even more dangerous than you used to be," she said softly. "There seems to be something about you and cars. Maybe an acquired weakness."

He caught her hand, braided their fingers together. "Are you? Acquiring an old weakness, Kara?"

Her fingers tightened in his. Her whisper was suddenly hoarse with honesty. "What I am . . . is scared. Scared of losing my head, with a man I'm not so positive I know anymore. You're stronger than the man I knew. Stronger, more sure, deeper on the inside." She hesitated, her heart in her eyes. "And the fire's stronger than it was. The fire, the magic—it's not just sexual feelings. I wish it were as easy as sex."

Through the slush of rain, something gleamed white and metallic. "Kara—"

"We didn't make time for each other before. We forgot to talk. We know what went wrong now, and when we're together . . . I feel something wonderful, a sense of rightness and completeness I never felt before—''

"Sunshine—''

"But I'm still afraid. Of us, of you. When we were teenagers, you were my dark prince, my forbidden lover. You swept me away. Only we're not teenagers now, and, Reardon, you're still trying to sweep me away. And I'm just not sure how you're going to feel when reality hits. . . .''

"Karen." His fingers curled around her chin because he couldn't snag her attention any other way. As badly as he wanted to respond to her feelings, her fears, at that specific moment, reality had already hit. He gently turned her chin toward the foggy rain-rivuleted window.

"There's another car out there,'' she noticed vaguely.

"Teenagers have a way of finding secluded spots,'' he agreed.

"But it's a white car.''

"Yes.''

"A white . . . Cherokee. Like yours. Amazingly . . . like yours.''

Craig swiped a hand over his eyes. "Kara. It *is* mine. And that's our son. With a girl. And, honey, the last thing I want to do is cut off this conversation, but—''

"Jon Jacob?" Karen reared off his lap like a horse at the starting gate. "It couldn't be.'' She pressed her nose to the glass, then jerked back. "Tarnation. It is.'' The mixture of comical disbelief and panic in her eyes

almost made him laugh. "We'll talk some other time," she informed him.

"I came to that same conclusion."

"You think he recognized us?"

Craig shook his head. "Your Cierra is a common make and color. It's raining and it's dark, and I suspect his attention is temporarily. . . elsewhere."

Her maternal antenna was already tuned to that channel. "Our son is *not* old enough to neck."

"Ah, honey? He's old enough."

"I think that's something else we'd better talk about another time."

"I agree." He watched her lips purse in a schoolmarm line.

"How could this possibly be happening to us? *Again?* I'm getting too old for this kind of life, Clyde," she said crisply.

"Now, Bonnie, we're getting pretty good at these getaways."

"This one's on you. You're driving." She scrambled over him, changing places with elbow-bumping haste. "Don't turn on the lights until you have to, then hit the gas and don't stop until we hit the border."

"Yes, ma'am."

A black satin slip, a scarlet camisole and a pale peach teddy draped on hangers in the dressing room at Rafter's.

The department store at the mall was Julie's hangout, not Karen's, but when her daughter headed into the next dressing room with an armload of clothes, she scooped up a few things to try on to wile away the time.

Once in the dressing room, though, she shook her head in bemusement. Her mind was obviously in the clouds. She should have looked before she "scooped." Truthfully she needed some lingerie, but there was no point in trying on any of these things. She fingered the slinky black satin slip...thinking that it was hardly her style...thinking that she was terrifyingly in love with her ex-husband.

Two days had passed since their "getaway." A hundred times she'd told herself that the situation had never been funny. The risk of getting caught in a compromising position by their sixteen-year-old son was the stuff of anxiety, not humor. Still. In times of trouble, when all the chips went down, Karen had long discovered that a sense of humor was the glue that could hold two people together.

Laughter was one of the bonds they'd lost. The ability to laugh at life. At each other. With each other.

She closed her eyes, feeling a surge of huge emotion swell in her throat. It wasn't just the bond of laughter she was rediscovering with Craig. It was everything. It was feeling punch-drunk with anticipation when she knew they would be together, and feeling on fire every time he touched her. It was discovering that she *liked* the man he'd become, his quiet confidence, his sneaky humor and subtle perception, his natural style. She liked his smile. She liked the way his eyes crinkled at the corners. She liked...

"Mom? Like, are you daydreaming, or what? I've been talking to you for ages—"

Karen's eyes shot open. "I'm sorry, sweetheart." Abruptly she turned back into "Mom." Pushing aside the dressing-room curtain, she studied the outfit Julie had tried on. "It looks good."

Julie spun around in a circle. "You don't think it's too long?"

"Maybe an inch. But the fabric's easy to shorten."

"You think the color makes me look washed-out?"

"I think you look wonderful in that soft blue. And it'll wash like a dream. If you like it, we'll get it."

Julie cautiously admitted, "It's not on sale."

"That's okay."

Her daughter's eyes widened in shock. "Mom, you're obviously not yourself today...." Her gaze strayed from her mother's face to the hanging lingerie. "Geezle-beezle. You're not going to buy any of that stuff, are you?"

Of course not. The words were on the tip of her tongue, yet she glanced again at the scraps of lace and satin. They were so pretty. She'd always been too practical, too sensible, too responsible to indulge in sexy underthings. Or maybe she'd just never had the courage? "I think," she said thoughtfully, "I may."

"You have to be kidding. Mom, that stuff just isn't you," Julie sternly informed her.

"Hmm." While Julie was changing, she figured she'd make up her mind. "Come on, you. Shake a leg and get dressed. I'll spring for the blue outfit. And you still have time to hit the tape store before we have to head for home. I need some things from the drugstore."

Normally they would have separated for a stretch to do their individual shopping. To be publicly seen with one's mother was not always cool. Yet once they left the store and joined the mainstream of mall traffic, Julie stuck closer than glue.

"I've been meaning to talk to you for the whole past week."

"About?"

Julie roped an arm around her mother's neck. "Mom... you wouldn't be trying to keep anything from me, would you? Like, for the sake of a really crazy example... you wouldn't be interested in somebody without telling me? Like a guy?"

To protect her daughter from potential harm, Karen thought she'd do just about anything. Lie, cheat, steal, or in this case, equivocate. "Sweetheart, is there some special reason this is on your mind?"

"No, not exactly. It's just that I was thinking. Like, you haven't gone out with anyone since Dad. If you were gonna do something like that, I think you should talk with me first. And another thing."

Her fifteen-year-old had suddenly developed eyes older than time. Karen wasn't sure she was ready to hear "another thing."

"Just for the record... I mean, for the sake of conversation and all that... you wouldn't marry somebody that Jon and I didn't like, would you?"

Karen squeezed her daughter in a quick hug. "Never in this life," she said sincerely. "And that's a promise you can take to the bank, petunia."

Julie, reassured, bounced off for the music store at an exuberant jog. Karen stared after her, momentarily charmed and disarmed by the cross between urchin and worldly-wise woman that her daughter had become... but also concerned.

Both kids had been behaving strangely, and now Julie was asking questions about men. If the children couldn't *know* she was seeing Craig, they were both smart. Too smart to keep a secret from them for long.

Yet the reason Karen so strongly wanted her relationship with Craig kept secret had been in her daughter's eyes. Julie was possessive of her. Protective. Probably more than was natural or healthy. It was one of the effects of the divorce. Both kids worried too much about her, about Craig, about adult problems. And for them to build a bubble of hope of a reconciliation... Karen refused to risk hurting them again.

A carrot-topped urchin raced past her, giggling and laughing. With a smile, Karen sidestepped out of his way, but her heart was suddenly pounding, pounding. For weeks now, Craig had been courting her like a lover. For weeks, she'd tasted the promise of hope and the rich, sweet fullness of rediscovering love again. In so many ways, he'd shown her that he'd changed.

But there was no denying that their new relationship had developed at a roller-coaster pace. And what Craig felt... she wasn't so sure of. He wanted her. She'd have to be blind not to know that his physical desire for her was real. Every moment between them was stolen, special, electric. Yet that kind of excitement was also the taproot of her anxiety.

It was fun stealing kisses in the attic. Hiding out. Cocooning themselves in a world of two. It was the same black magic they'd discovered when they were kids. The rekindling of old memories, the flirting with a little danger, the romance of meeting in secret . . . tarnation, they'd both been overserious, over-responsible workaholics for years. It *was* fun.

But it wasn't real life.

Remembering that, every time, was where Karen got scared. Real life was where they'd bogged down before. Lightning never lasted forever. The strongest sizzles had a way of petering out when the daily routine came down to buying groceries and taking out the trash.

The most crippling wound of the divorce, for her, had been the feelings of failure and inadequacy in herself as a woman. She'd loved him, but she hadn't been able to hold his interest, and ultimately she was still Karen, still the woman he'd been married to for seventeen years.

There was a wildflower that grew high in the mountains. It looked like a weed during the day. Its petals only opened at night, and then the flower unfurled a lush exotic scent as intoxicating as the moonlight. The wildflower was like her and Craig, their relationship a secret romance by moonlight.

But how could she possibly be sure that his feelings were strong enough to endure the harsh light of day?

Eight

It was past 10:00 p.m. when the phone rang. Karen upended her book and reached over the pillows for the receiver on the bedside table.

"Kara? When Jon was over this afternoon, we ended up having quite a talk. I found out about the girl he was with the other night."

Karen drew up her knees under the covers. At the first sound of Craig's voice, her pulse picked up a steady hum. "Tell me."

"Her name's Marsha."

"Never heard of her."

"No surprise," Craig murmured dryly. "I don't think she's exactly the kind of girl Jon Jacob was gonna bring home to meet you. She sounds faster than a greyhound and a lot more wild. It seems she's been chasing our son for more than a year and finally cornered him into taking her out. First date. She was the one who suggested parking, and then—I gathered from the color of your son's face when he was talking about it—she was all over him like a blanket on a bed.''

"Yikes."

Craig chuckled. "That sounded like a pretty maternal 'yikes.' Our son was coming from a slightly different perspective. I think he saw it as being helpless in the clutches of a brazen hussy. Every boy's favorite fantasy come true. Anyway, I know you were worried that he recognized your car and was just keeping quiet about it, but, honestly, I doubt it."

"Forget *that* worry. Good grief. Do you think that he ... that they ... ?"

"No. Actually, I think she scared him witless. This is the day of AIDS, my son informs me, and I gather this little sweetheart has not only been around the block, she's halfway through the football team. Some of your lectures on sexual responsibility must have gotten through, sunshine. But—"

"But what?"

She could hear him shifting the receiver against his ear, guessed he was settling into the oversize leather chair in his living room. "But he just grew up five years. It's been a while since he volunteered for a major man-to-man talk, but this was something he couldn't hold in. We're talking a swelled chest and a masculine ego tattooed on his forehead. She *wanted* him. Like a woman wants a man. You've just never been a sixteen-year-old boy, Kara. That's the headiest thing you can imagine."

Karen glanced up and nearly had a heart attack when she realized Julie was standing in the doorway. She clapped a palm over the receiver. Her daughter waved a hello with a half-eaten apple, her dark eyes bright with curiosity. "It's so late. I just wondered who was calling you."

Karen said, "Mr. Macalvey. From work. He couldn't find some files we were working on." Julie scrunched up her nose in sympathy, took another crunch of the apple and waved her a good-night. Karen waited to snug the receiver to her ear until Julie was down the hall, yet Craig must have heard.

"Macalvey, hmm? You're in bed, aren't you?"

"Yes, Mr. Macalvey." Beneath the covers, her toes were suddenly curling. He'd called to confide information about their fast-maturing teenage son. That natural sharing and sense of connection had made her feel good... but now he was done talking about Jon Jacob. His tone rolled out like a smoky sax in a late-night bar.

"White sheets?"

"Pink."

"And you're wearing a T-shirt. I'll bet... Broncos. And nothing beneath it?"

Although he couldn't know it, she was wearing a Broncos T-shirt with nothing underneath. And her heart was suddenly beating like a clock with a manic battery. He'd done it twice this week. Called her late in the evening. And bedeviled her with that voice. Beguiled her with wicked nonsense until her body was so churned up she couldn't sleep.

"I can picture those long slim legs sliding on those smooth sheets. I love your legs, honey. You can't imagine how much they've been on my mind. I keep remembering the shape of your calf, your thigh, the feel of you through those silk stockings. Do you have any idea how hot I was for you? Bare, though, Kara. Bare would be so much better...."

A squeak escaped her throat. It wasn't Julie in the doorway this time, but Jon Jacob, silently juggling a pair of tennis balls. He dropped one when he realized he had her attention, and bounded in the room to fetch it. When she clutched the receiver to her chest, he shrugged sheepishly.

"I just wanted to know if everything was okay. It's pretty late for anybody to be calling you."

Karen cleared the rattle from her throat. "Everything's fine. It's just Mr. Macalvey from work. He was in the office late and had a question about some things we were working on."

When Jon Jacob was gone, Karen scrunched down against the pillows and hugged the telephone close. "Mr. Macalvey?"

"Yes, ma'am?"

"You're shameless and you're bad and the entire world is awake in this house, so this conversation is over. But I just want you to know...I'm gonna get you for this. I don't know how. And I don't know when. But if I were you, I'd start feeling real, real nervous."

She heard him chuckle as she severed the connection. A moment later, she reached over to flick off the bedside lamp. Her room dipped in darkness, although the kids were still up. Water was running in the bathroom. A radio played rock real low. Another fifteen minutes passed before the hall light went out and the children settled down. Finally it was completely dark. And totally quiet.

She grabbed a pillow and hugged it to her chest, nowhere near sleeping. Beneath the sheets, she was conscious of her bare legs against the cool percale, and her breasts felt sensitized and heavy. Because of him. Her skin felt on fire. Because of him.

The dreadful man had the unprincipled nerve to remind her of her sinfully abandoned behavior in the car. Worse yet, he'd loved doing it, loved teasing her, and knowing she had to be careful of every word she'd said had doubtless prodded his wicked sense of humor. It was the kind of lovers' game he loved. The kind of lovers' game *she* loved.

And the kind of excitement that had completely disappeared from their marriage in the last years before the divorce.

Her mood sobering, Karen climbed out of bed and restlessly paced to the moonlit window. The fear crept up on her again, gnawing at her heart, that Craig was caught up in the heady tailspin of lovers' games and the power of old memories. Falling in love was wonderful. Loving, the kind of loving that lasted, had to be tested and grounded in real life. Would Craig still want her when the secret fireworks were over?

She touched the cool windowpane, and stared down at the silent yard glistening with frost. *Who's fault was it that the fireworks disappeared from the relationship to begin with, Kara?*

Fragments of their conversation about Jon Jacob drifted back through her mind. *Helpless in the clutches of a brazen hussy. Every man's favorite fantasy.* All Craig had been doing was offering her a man's perspective on their teenage son, but his comments bit. Seventeen years together, yet she hadn't known that was a favorite fantasy of his. How could a lover not know such a basic thing about her mate?

She'd never been a "hussy." It just wasn't in her character. Craig had always been the seducer in their bed. In the heat of passion, she lost her inhibitions—they'd always come together with equal fire—so who initiated their lovemaking never seemed to matter.

Karen wrapped her arms around her chest—achingly tight. It *did* matter. Variety was spice. Heaven knew, Craig had openly reveled in her responsiveness, but even the most ardent seducer could tire of a repetitive aggressive role.

Too rarely, Karen thought, had she been sensitive to his needs.

If she was honestly afraid to trust Craig's feelings, he'd been pursuing her—she couldn't doubt—from the heart. In a dozen ways, he'd tried to show her that he wouldn't repeat his past mistakes. Now it struck her that she needed to face up to where she'd failed him, and herself, the first time around.

It had always been easy to let him take the lead, because she was uncomfortable in an assertive role. It had been easy to blame him for taking her for granted, when she'd sat still and let that happen. It had been easy, damn easy, to stand in his shadow, because he was a strong, sure, take-charge kind of man. And she'd never been that sure of herself as a woman.

The bottom line was inescapable. She'd better *get* sure. If she loved him, she'd damn well better find the guts, and the confidence, to fight for him.

* * *

A sedate and prim-faced secretary led Craig into the inner sanctum of a dark paneled office. As he strode in, he straightened his tie—and his chin—thinking that he'd rather chew nails than be anywhere near here.

"Craig." It was a greeting of sorts, but the tall, austere man behind the cluttered desk neither stood, nor offered a hand. The secretary closed the door, leaving them alone. Karen's father motioned him to one of the upholstered chairs opposite the desk. "I haven't talked with you in a long time."

"I know." Craig lowered himself in the nearest chair, aware of exactly how much time had passed since he'd had a private conversation with Walt Hennessey. They'd seen each other in the process of dropping off or picking up grandkids, but that was the sum total of their contact for more than a year. Craig assumed that Karen's father blamed him for the divorce, blamed him, from the start, for getting his youngest and dearest in trouble.

It wasn't, and never had been, a comfortable relationship.

Karen looked like her mother, not her dad. Walt had an angular face, a head of balding brown hair, and was wearing a tailored and expensive gray suit that hung on his lean frame like cheap curtains. Suits just didn't fit him. Fishing clothes and a cigar fit him. Image wasn't a problem that concerned Walt. He was one of the best tax attorneys in the state; he was shrewd, smart, intuitive and tough at a gut level.

And Karen loved her dad like she loved no one else in this life, at a heart level. Which was why Craig had decided—even if the older man greeted him with a guillotine—that this one-on-one was necessary. And he still believed that, but Walt was patiently studying him like a cop with a handcuffed suspect.

Craig didn't see any choice but to plunge in. "Your daughter would likely shoot me if she knew I was here, but I want you to know. I'm seeing Karen again."

Silence. But at least no hand grenades or dueling swords showed up on the desk. Karen's father simply quietly drummed his fingers on the edge of the chair. "I suppose... I suspected. You didn't telephone at home, didn't come to the house. There could only be so many reasons why you would have arranged a private meeting in my office."

"Yes."

"Erica will raise holy hell if she discovers you're anywhere near our daughter again." Walt didn't pull his punches.

Neither did Craig. "I know."

"The children?"

Craig shook his head. "No. They don't know what's going on. Neither do my parents or friends or anyone else. Karen wants it that way—no one involved until we're both sure of a reconciliation. She wants to protect the kids. Her mother. You. And I agree with her... except about you."

He unbuttoned his suit coat and hunched forward. "You know damn well that I sneaked around with Karen when we were kids. And it bothered me that if you found out I was seeing her on the quiet, you'd think I was doing the same thing. I'm not asking your permission or expecting your approval, Walt. I'm just telling you straight that I love your daughter and I'm hoping to win her back."

Walt stopped drumming his fingers. "You keep looking at me like you expect me to pull out a horse-whip," he remarked dryly.

"Maybe that's what I'd do if I were in your shoes."

Karen's father almost smiled. "Don't think I didn't consider it, when you were both seventeen. But that's water—and a lot of years—over the dam." He picked up a pencil and tapped it on his desk, end to end. "You never gave me the chance to say this before, but I never blamed you—or her—for the divorce. I never knew what went wrong, but I watched you both in hell that last year. Even looking at Karen used to tear at my heart. And maybe you thought I didn't notice, but I had some real fears that the father of my grandchildren was damn close to cracking up."

Craig had expected, been prepared for, almost anything from Walt Hennessey but compassion. "Maybe I almost did," he admitted, and then hesitated. He'd come here for Kara, not because he owed anything to Walt. But being a father himself now, he couldn't seem to just up and leave without saying something more.

"When I was in school," he said slowly, "I was a golden boy. Good in athletics. Not bad in looks. A quick enough mind to bring down grades without opening a book. No hardships, except for my parents splitting up." He lifted a hand, palm out, in a gesture of blunt honesty. "There was no depth. Not when I met Kara, not for years after that. I just assumed I could have anything I wanted, because that's what I grew up believing. I wasn't spoiled in the sense of a kid who had too much. But life did a good job of spoiling me, because everything came easy. So if you wanted to know what went wrong—it was me. Not Kara. I was selfish and arrogant and I took her for granted."

The phone buzzed on Walt's desk. He punched the button, picked up the receiver and said politely, "I'm not here, Mrs. Rivers." Then hung up the phone. Afternoon sunlight streamed from the open window behind him, highlighting the creases of age on his face. The pencil in his hands lay still.

"You've come a long way from that boy you used to be," he said finally.

"I'm hoping to convince your daughter of that."

"A lion's job. In thirty-six years, I've never been able to convince my daughter of anything," Walt said dryly, and then paused. "If this reconciliation were set in granite, I doubt you would be here. So Karen isn't as sure as you?"

The question rattled all the caged nerves in his stomach. Craig said quietly, "I *love* her." It was the only answer he had, and not near enough, he thought, to satisfy a father.

Yet Walt relaxed in his chair and abruptly moved the conversation along. "If and when you're both sure... I'll handle her mother. And in the meantime, I could occasionally take the kids off your hands. They're getting so grown-up that they rarely have time for a grandpa anymore, but I could still finagle them into an outing or two. Football tickets. Riding. I'd think of something."

Craig cleared his throat. "Whether you believe it or not, I didn't come here for your support. I only told you the situation to be sure you were in Kara's corner, no matter what happened."

"Unnecessary. I was always in my daughter's corner. Nothing she could possibly do would ever change that." He added thoughtfully, "You know, when she was growing up, the boys flocked around her like flies. If there wasn't one on the phone, there was one hanging around the porch or blocking the driveway with some pitiful-looking jalopy. But from the time you two met, that was it for her. And although I doubt I could convince you to believe it, Craig, I always thought she made a damn good choice." Walt cocked his head and said amiably, "But if you hurt her again, I swear to God I'll see your neck in a noose."

Craig stood. He said quietly, "I'll buy the noose."

Predictably, when he was late, there wasn't a green light in all of Colorado Springs. The instant the red light turned, Craig pushed the accelerator to the floor. Traffic didn't thin out until he reached Wildwood. The air smelled like fall, chipper and brisk, but sun grazed down on the cache of homes on their hillside suburb. It was 12:07 now. He was due to meet Kara at his place at noon sharp, because neither of them could spare more than an hour from the workday.

He checked his appearance in the rearview mirror and swore. He looked as if he'd been battling wolves all morning, which he had—wolves of the corporate species. As he braked in the drive—her Cierra was already there—he simultaneously tried to straighten his tie, divest his pocket of three pens and a memo and finger shovel his hair into some claim to neatness.

More relevant, he mentally ran through the conversation he wanted to have with her. The meeting yesterday with her father still clung to his conscience.

Walt had been unexpectedly supportive to the ex-son-in-law who had a disastrously long history of getting his daughter in trouble. It should have relieved Craig's mind.

Instead he'd found himself going to bed last night and sleeping with guilt.

He'd been steamrollering Kara. And knew it. The book, the flowers, the phone calls, the sneaked encounters in attics and dark corners and cars, the pressure—the seductive, sexual pressure—to remember how good they could be together. He *wanted* her. Not just in his bed, but in his life. Permanently in his life.

But Walt had indirectly implied what shape Karen had been in around the time of the divorce, that her confidence had shattered with the failure of the marriage. And Craig knew well that she was still vulnerable.

To risk hurting her—no matter how much he loved her, no matter how sure he was that a reconciliation would work—was beyond unconscionable. He had to slow down. He had to slow *them* down, and give Kara time. It had only been a month. She couldn't possibly trust him that quickly.

As he strode up the walk, Craig mentally vowed that this would be a nice, easy, relaxed lunch for Karen. They'd talk. Nothing more. He'd be a gentleman, no push, no pressure, with all traces of steamrollering obliterated from his character and his hormones under lock and key.

He leapt up the two steps to the porch of his adobe ranch. After the divorce, Karen and the kids had stayed in "their" house. Craig had bought the first property for sale in the same neighborhood, and the house was small, cramped and inconveniently laid-out. His need to be physically close to the kids had been his only motivation, he'd thought then. Mutual custody had never been a theoretical term to him. A year ago, the proximity to Karen had never crossed his mind as a mitigating factor.

But it was.

He pushed open the front door, calling her name. Earlier on the phone, she'd said her boss was gone for the day and she'd easily have time to pick up Chinese. A good thing, because he'd never caught a spare minute to breathe all morning.

Karen didn't immediately answer. He was about to call her name again when he spotted her shoes. Killer heels, black with white toes, lying one and then the other like a Hansel-and-Gretel trail on his gray carpet.

The steel-gray carpet was as bland and dark as his whole living room, relieved only by the kids' electronics. The room had been decorated by gadgetry. A sound system. A big screen TV. A computer stand and table, piled high with programs, discs, a mouse and computer paraphernalia. It was all stuff for the kids; Craig rarely even sat in the room.

The kids always left debris. Julie had left a tape, nail polish and a powder-blue sweatshirt when she'd been here last. They were still heaped in a pile on the gun-metal gray couch. The football stashed in the corner, gathering dust, also the "cool" pair of shades and some old school papers, were Jon Jacob's.

Craig saw those, but his gaze riveted on a red jacket. A raw-silk red jacket that had been tossed, with abandoned neglect, on his only easy chair.

Still walking, he discovered another item of clothing in the hall between the living room and kitchen. It was a tasteful, demure, subtle black dress. Long sleeved. High in the neck. Suitable for an office, nothing suggestive about it.

Except that it wasn't on a body. It was lying in a puddle on his hall carpet.

Craig opened his mouth to call for Karen again, only the sudden frog in his throat had short-circuited his vocal chords. He cleared his throat. Still nothing came out.

He took a cautious step toward the kitchen and almost immediately heard her humming. When he turned the corner he found her. The kitchen was narrow and long, with terra-cotta tiles and cream walls and an island counter that divided the room. In the morning he had coffee at the kitchen table, but overall the surface was a stash-all for mail, work projects and tools midway to being put away. The counter was set up with bar stools, where he usually grabbed a meal.

"Craig!" Karen whirled around. Her hand splayed to her throat when she spotted him. "You scared me! I didn't hear you come in." Her grin was winsome and welcoming. Nothing to suggest that anything was out of the ordinary. "It's your own fault if you don't like lunch. You're late."

"I...um...couldn't help it." He couldn't move the frog in his throat for love or money.

She motioned to the food spread out on the island counter. "I know I told you I'd bring in Chinese, but this seemed easier. Nothing to heat up or cook, nothing to clean up. All we need is some paper plates and our fingers.''

He could see that. It was all finger foods set out picnic-style. Fresh raw shrimp, white and cold, with a cocktail sauce. Tiny wedged sandwiches, dozens of them, all bite-size. An artfully arranged plate of vegetables included artichoke hearts, an old favorite of his. A cup held toothpicks. Nothing required a fork. Even, he noticed, the tiny glass bowl in the center that was filled with wet, red maraschino cherries.

"It looks...fine," he said.

"I had fun putting it together. The only problem is that eating with our hands is likely to be a little messy. That's no sweat for you as it's your house and you could easily change your shirt if you had to. But I didn't have that luxury.''

It was hard, very hard, for him to tear his gaze from that bowl of maraschino cherries, but apparently Karen was trying to logically and sensibly explain why she'd stripped off her office clothes. He could well understand that she didn't want to risk going back to work with a cocktail-sauce stain on her dress. Finger foods *were* messy.

"Sit down, sit down," she scolded him. "I don't know about you, but I had a heckuva morning. I definitely need this hour to put my feet up. The afternoon's likely to be even worse...."

She gave him a cheerful rundown of her beleaguered morning, relating anecdotes to make him laugh. He plunked down on the bar stool, grateful for that solid contact with reality, and cupped his chin in his hand. Karen whisked past him. Iced tea appeared with a wedge of lime. "Where do you keep your napkins? I can't find a darn thing in this kitchen...." But she found the napkins and whisked past him again. He caught the drift of her perfume, something spicy and exotic and alarming. Extremely alarming. She'd never worn the scent before, at least not around him.

"Now..." A frown pinched her forehead. For a spare two seconds, she stopped all the frenetic motion and plopped her fists on her hips. "What else do we need? I know, I just know, I've forgotten something...." She met his eyes, but only briefly.

Craig guessed she didn't have the nerve to meet his eyes for more than briefly.

She was wearing a slip and stockings. Technically the slip covered the same territory that her usual practical, modest lingerie covered. Only not in the same way. The slip was black. Satin. The scalloped hem reached midthigh. The two straps were skinnier than pencils. The shiny, slinky fabric clung to her figure, dipping low at her breasts, hugging the curve of her hips. She wasn't wearing a bra. Her nipples, tight as rosebuds, poked distinctly through the thin material. And from the outline of tiny bumps at the tops of her thighs, he guessed she wasn't wearing panty hose but using garters to hold up her stockings. Black satin garters.

"Karen," he said, "Sit down."

"I'm sure I've forgotten something—"

"Kara. Sit. Down."

Nine

"Karen... I feel I've been rushing you. Unfairly. I've even been using the chemistry between us unfairly—"

Karen dipped a chilled shrimp in the cocktail sauce and wedged it between his lips. Craig clearly needed immediate sustenance. He was stumbling over his words. His face was flushed with color.

It was the first time she had ever seen him shocked. At least, shocked by her. All morning she'd fretted and worried whether she could pull this off. Playing out Craig's secret fantasy about the brazen hussy—he knew her too well; it wouldn't work; it just wasn't her. She'd been afraid of feeling foolish. Of looking foolish.

But his response, from the instant he walked in the kitchen, had plumped up her confidence... and fueled her determination. Maybe he'd seen her in a lot less than a slip, but he'd never seen her like this. All those years. Who would have guessed she had the feminine power to make him so nervous?

She pushed the last of the tidbit in his mouth. Given no choice, his teeth closed on the succulent white meat of the shrimp. "Neither of us ever had control over that chemistry," she crooned. "Be careful with the sauce, honey. It's . . . hot."

She shifted on the bar stool, crossing her legs. His gaze dived to her legs, then to the swell of her breasts straining against the black satin edge when she leaned closer. Before lunch, she'd stopped at Keastman's. The expensive department store sold Gucci One, which she couldn't conceivably afford, but they kept a sample spray bottle on the counter. Whether Craig liked the view or the scent, it was hard to say. But he swallowed the bite of shrimp in a lump. And his other hand reached out to unchoke the tie at his neck. "Kara?"

"Hmm?"

"I'm trying to be serious."

"Me, too. I'm in a very serious mood," she assured him.

"I don't want you to feel pushed . . . into a decision . . . into feelings . . . without all the time you need to be sure. Honestly sure—"

With a duly serious expression, she hand-fed him another fat, juicy shrimp. "Chew this one slowly," she suggested. "Real slowly. Let the taste burst on your tongue . . . cool and cold. Compared to the sauce—"

"I know. The sauce is hot," he said hoarsely.

An ebony clasp pulled back her hair. She unclipped it and shook her hair loose. The strands cascaded in a wanton fall to her bare shoulders. She smiled at Craig.

Two dots of moisture appeared on his brow. He closed his eyes.

"You haven't tried an artichoke yet."

"I don't want to try an artichoke."

"Sure, you do. You love them, and it'll be a soothing taste after all that hot sauce. A softer taste. Milder. It'll melt on your tongue like a dip into honey...." His eyes opened again, dark and razor bright, when she fed him a bite of an artichoke heart.

"Kara?"

"Yes?"

"I'm trying to talk to you. I'm trying to talk *honestly* with you."

"Verbal communication is important," she agreed, but thought, *Not just then.* The other night, she'd been right. This was one of the ingredients that had been left out of the recipe before. Even when chemistry was powerful, excitement dulled when there was never a dose of surprise. Maybe she'd known that before, but she'd never pushed herself into experimenting with a more assertive role—in bed or anywhere else. She'd been too afraid of looking foolish in his eyes, too afraid of failing him. And herself.

In a life-threatening situation, she obviously wanted him to feel sure of her. In a life-threatening situation, she wanted to be sure of Craig.

But as for being sure what he was going to be fed for lunch ... she glanced at the muscle ticking like a little time bomb in his jaw. And thought, *Lord, Reardon. You're never getting Campbell's soup from me again.*

"Karen ..."

"Hmm?" She watched him take a long deep breath. He was having a terrible time concentrating—although he gave it one last valiant try.

"I heard what you said. The other night. About worrying that we were living out old memories, by meeting secretly, by being swept away. I don't want you feeling swept away. That is...I do. I liked it, as a man, that I could still make you feel that way. But as far as confusing the past and present, I never..." A long pause. His narrowed gaze followed the trail of her slim hand, extending across the counter, scooping a single red cherry from the glass bowl and lifting it, dripping, to her lips. Her white teeth sank into the luscious sweetness.

"Hell," he said thickly.

Her brows arched in surprise at the flat expletive.

"Damn it, do you think I'm made of steel?"

She shook her head no.

"You set up this lunch looking for trouble."

She nodded her head yes.

"You *love* trouble."

She nodded again.

"Well, now you're gonna get it." His hand closed on her wrist just as she was innocently reaching for another cherry. The bar stool spun when he yanked her off it and pulled her behind him. Wherever they were headed, they seemed to be traveling faster than bank robbers chased by a posse.

Once midway down the hall, though, and away from the overbright windows, he stopped and hauled her close. Haste of a different kind seemed to overtake his mood. His hands streaked the length of her black satin slip, kneading her spine, cupping her to him with blatant hunger. He buried her mouth under his in a series of wooing kisses, carnal kisses, embezzling kisses that threatened to ransom her ability to think.

But not completely. She pushed the jacket from his shoulders and, when he lifted his head for air, fumbled with the buttons on his white shirt. His tie bobbed in her way, making her chuckle. When she saw the heat percolating in his eyes, the laughter died in her throat, replaced by a softer, darker emotion that locked all the oxygen in her lungs.

It wasn't a lust attack she saw in his face, but a love attack. Enchantment of the most magical kind. Longing and belonging made volatile by passion, made richer and more dangerous by desire.

Slowly, aware he was watching her, she unfastened the last of his shirt buttons and pulled the white linen fabric free. Her fingers scalloped a path up his brown chest, over hard muscle and through wiry, springy hair. Tension vibrated off his skin. His heart galloped when the pads of her thumbs rubbed over his nipples. He sucked in air, a rasping gulp of it, when her arms wound around his neck and her breasts snugged against his chest. Technically, a wisp of slippery cool satin separated them. It wasn't much of a technicality, and the satin didn't stay cool long.

His voice sounded as if he'd swallowed an entire cup of molasses. "You keep this up, sunshine, and we'll be making love in the hall."

"I'm afraid that has to be your problem," she murmured. "I'm busy." She snagged open his leather belt, then tilted her head, looking at him through a sweep of lashes as she pulled the belt free. "You're snared in the clutches of a wanton hussy, Reardon. Brace yourself, because there's just nothing you can do. I'm gonna sweep you away."

"I like this fantasy."

"I thought you might."

"But do you think there's any chance..." His whisper was rough, said between kisses delivered to the curve of her neck. Kisses that made her shiver. "That I could participate in this seduction?"

"No." She had to be firm.

"No?"

"No. I decided..." For an instant, when his cheek nuzzled the slope of her shoulder, she forgot what she'd decided. Then it came back. "I decided that I like it. Your being in my clutches. My helpless kidnappee. Maybe...I'll make you be patient for a long, long time."

Maybe not.

His hands tangled in her hair, anchoring her for an openmouthed kiss that was hotter than steam and as possessive as a brand. He walked her backward without breaking the kiss. He shucked off one shoe, then the other, without breaking the kiss. When they stopped moving, she vaguely noticed chocolate sheets and vanilla blankets and the barren expanse of a king-size bed within pouncing distance. Mostly she noticed that her kidnappee was cooperating in his unwilling seduction by pushing off his suit pants and underwear in a blur of speed.

Then he came for her. Slowly he peeled down the spaghetti straps of the slip, exposing her taut swollen breasts for his eyes, then just as slowly let the satin fabric slither over her hips and pool at her feet. She still wore stockings and a black lace garter belt. But nothing else.

She'd never before had a fear of heights, but the look in his eyes gave her a dizzying attack of vertigo. The next thing she knew, he'd lifted her to the center of the fuzzy vanilla blankets and covered her with his weight, his mouth, his hands.

His palm cupped her breast, plumping the soft white flesh, his thumb working the dark rose tip until she hurt. A hot, sweet, terrible hurt. He unsnapped the garters and rolled down the stockings, chasing them down her legs with a trail of velvet kisses, creating another hot, sweet, terrible hurt.

She'd made love with him a zillion times. But not like this. They'd set off rockets in the cabin that early morning in September. Even then . . . not like this.

Desire had been building all these weeks, but there'd been no time before, no private time. To revel in the feel of him. To look her fill. To explore, with no fear of discovery, the newness of her lover, the newness of emotions toward this man she once thought she knew.

His skin grew slick. Hers slippery. Even a frenzy of touching couldn't slake her thirst. Every taste, touch, sound seemed to magnify his. She wanted him with a longing that sprang straight from her soul. Somewhere there was sun, beating through a slatted shade. And a fuzzy blanket crumpled, rumpled, in their way. All she knew was the blaze of heat, stemming from him, seeping through her liquid limbs like wet fire.

Craig lifted his head. His eyes, as glazed as ebony, raked her tumbled damp hair, her bruised lips, her trapped breathing. Without breaking her gaze, he yanked open a drawer in the bedside table, fumbled for a foil packet. "Did you think I'd risk you, sunshine?" he whispered.

His lips touched hers, more than a kiss, but a sharing of poignant intimacy, for all they'd been together... for all they could be. She tasted his love as surely as the force of his desire. And then he pulled her arms around his neck and climbed on.

The ride was earthy and wicked and long, a soul-soaring pace, an emotional gallop across plains and peaks of sensation. Wonder filled her, a feeling of rightness so lancingly powerful that it eclipsed all else—but him. At the crest, just before pleasure shattered through both of them, she whispered, "I love you."

He'd heard her. If his conscience, that morning, had warned him not to rush her into making love, now Craig wished he'd hustled her into bed long before. If he'd known she was ready to say those three words, he would have.

Kara was curled around him like a drowsy, weakened kitten. He stroked her back, snuggling her closer, feeling protective and possessive and sky-high. Behind his closed lids, he could still see her wearing that damned slip and the smile of a brazen hussy and her eyes so vulnerable that he'd lost his head.

And his heart. There should be smoke around the bed, he mused, because they'd come together with that much sensual fire. Her responsiveness still had him reeling. The wildness and freedom and honesty she'd given him... it had to come from trust.

He didn't have a ring back on her finger yet, he reminded himself. And words of love spoken in passion were not the same thing as a commitment. But if he were careful, infinitely careful, to nourish her trust— if he made no more mistakes—he could surely coax her to believe in their future.

She stirred in his arms, burrowing her cheek in the crest of his shoulder. A languid stretch. A sleepy yawn. No sign of nerves yet, and before she could develop any, he wrapped her just a little closer.

"You remember our wedding night?" he murmured.

She tilted her head. Suddenly she wasn't so sleepy. "A disaster of epic proportions," she murmured back.

"No, Kara. Not all of it." The pad of his thumb traced her brow, the arch of her nose. "The first part was fun. I remember kidnapping you. The wild drive through the night. The justice of the peace. I remember your excitement, your nerves. Although I have to confess that isn't the part I remember the best...."

"Maybe we could talk about the weather," she suggested darkly.

He didn't want to talk about the weather. He scooched down, so he could be nose to nose with her on the same pillow. "I remember the exact moment when we had the marriage certificate in our hands—we were legal, it was done and neither of us had the least idea what to do then. We didn't have a place to go. We didn't have the brains to plan that far ahead." Soft, like the brush of wings, his thumb traced her bottom lip. "You hated that motel."

"It was pretty."

"It was a motel."

"We had to stop somewhere. We obviously couldn't keep driving all night—"

"It was a motel," he repeated gently, "and it made you feel sleazy. Eloping had been romantic, all that forbidden secrecy and racing through the night. But suddenly we were in a cold, impersonal motel room. And then, to add insult to injury, you discovered you had a problem and hid out in the bathroom."

"Reardon—" Her tone was repressive, but he saw the splash of color in her cheeks, the way her lips were fighting a smile.

"I kept asking what's wrong, what's wrong. Nothing, you kept saying. But you wouldn't come out. You were in there an hour, at *least*, before you finally dredged up the courage to tell me—"

"Reardon—"

"It was a singular experience. Being eighteen, on my wedding night, going back on the road to find some drugstore open that sold sanitary napkins—"

Apparently she had enough of being teased, because she abruptly smothered his face with a pillow. When he tugged it off—and ran a fingertip down her ribs—she made dire threats of retribution through a throat full of laughter. The tussle ended up with her draped on his chest and claiming she had him pinned.

He thought otherwise. The blanket of her soft bare body stoked new hunger, fresh desire. They'd come so far since that long-ago wedding night. He wanted her to remember. They'd weathered more than good times, but a hundred touchy, awkward moments. He wanted her to remember that, too... and thought she did. For an instant she was breathless, her eyes lush with emotion—love, laughter and the soft glow of yearning.

"Craig, I..." With trembling fingers, she touched his face. He was sure, dead sure, that she was gaining confidence in their future and was willing to talk about it. The moment was lost, though, when she happened to notice the clock over the edge of his shoulder. The loving sensuality in her expression abruptly changed to comical horror. "Eek."

He didn't need to read the clock dials to know the lunch hour had gotten away from them. Kara tried to do a push-up off his chest. He lazily tugged her back down. There was no way she was getting away from him now. "You're not going back to work."

"Craig, I *have* to. I already took off extra time this morning—"

"Call in. Tell them you have a case of ptomaine. Tell them you're in labor with twins. Tell them that a 747 crashed into your car. Some excuse will work. When's the last time you took off a day?"

"Unless the kids were sick, I've never taken off a day."

"Sunshine, you're worse than me." He shook his head in scolding reproof. "Even a pair of overresponsible workaholics should be able to play hooky for a few hours. The kids won't get off the school bus until then. And you and I have unfinished business."

"Unfinished business?"

Those Madonna-blue eyes, he discovered, weren't opposed to being tempted. Once sure that she wasn't going to fly, Craig climbed out of bed and disappeared toward the kitchen.

When he came back, his palm cupped the small glass bowl of maraschino cherries.

Her gaze shot from the cherries . . . to his face.

He took the telephone off the hook and closed the door.

Hands slung in her jacket pockets, Karen watched the kids disappear over the top of the ravine with her dad. Once, every fall, her parents came up to the cabin for a weekend. They'd only arrived an hour ago. The drive up had been noisy, with everyone talking at once, and then carting in food and gear had been a predictably hectic process. For the first time all afternoon, she had a moment for herself.

She heard the kids' distant laughter, saw the late-afternoon sun glitter like spangles through the pines, heard the breeze sifting leaves in the yard. Alone for these few minutes, her eyes turned dreamy, unfocused.

She missed him. Fiercely. Unreasonably.

She'd already told herself the obvious. They'd seen each other every day that week; she'd see him again on Monday. It was just a weekend. She should be deliriously glad of the short separation. Heaven knew, she needed the chance to catch her breath. Craig had been running her ragged.

Very ragged. A hopeless, helpless smile tipped the corners of her mouth. The devil had had a case of maraschino cherries delivered to the house, which was only one of his more terrible ideas. Every day they'd met for lunch at his house, only he'd locked his doors and unplugged his phones and then feasted on her instead of lunch. His hunger was unappeasable, his imagination completely out of control. Her confidence in herself as a woman had never been this singing, stinging high. He'd seen to it. She went back to the office with the energy of a wasted waif. He'd seen to that, too.

Craig was in love with her. Which he'd told her. In bed and out of it, and often ... often enough to make a believer out of a once-scared doubter.

The cabin's screen door clapped loudly. Karen twisted around and promptly shelved all thoughts of Craig for another time. Her mother stood on the porch, a slim figure in jeans and a sweatshirt, her unlined face prettier, Karen thought, than her own would ever be. This week Erica's hair was pale champagne.

"Are they gone?" her mom called out impatiently.

"Yes. But just for a short hike down to the creek and back. Dad swore he'd be back in a half hour to start the fire." Karen migrated toward the kitchen. Traditionally her dad roasted a chicken over an open fire and baked potatoes in the coals, leaving little for the women to fix beyond condiments and a dessert. But those chores still had to be done.

"Good." Her mother trailed behind her.

"Good?" Karen echoed.

"Good, I'm glad they're gone. Your father gave me strict instructions before we got here. I was supposed to 'let you be,' not poke or pry or finagle you into any serious discussions. I couldn't *wait* until he took the kids off. What's wrong?"

Karen felt a moment's unease, yet answered honestly. "Nothing's wrong. I can't imagine what Dad was talking about." She pulled out a plate and opened the refrigerator for relishes.

"Well, something put a bee in your father's bonnet, because he was determined that I not interfere. As if I'd interfere in any of my children's lives. You're all grown women, for heaven's sake.'' Erica Hennessey piled paper plates and cutlery on a tray, then asked delicately, ''Something with the kids? Jon Jacob having any trouble in school?''

''Nope. Both kids are doing great.'' She plopped cellophane bags of carrot and celery sticks on the counter, then the dip she'd made at home. Riffling through the shelves, she spotted a jar of olives. Black olives. She suddenly craved the taste like a desert dweller starved for water. Closing the refrigerator door with her hip, she popped two. Then another two.

''Your health, then. Is there something wrong that you're not telling me? You know Samantha tried to keep me from finding out about that cyst last year....''

Karen knew about Sam's cyst. She also knew why her older sister had tried to keep the information from their mother. Erica Hennessey was a chronic worrier, especially when the subject was her daughters.

By the time Karen finished arranging the plate of vegetables and dip, they'd run through her mother's whole familiar list of prying questions. Her three sisters were quick to lose patience. Not Karen. From understanding came compassion. Her mom had always ruled the household with a nosy finger in every pie. With the girls grown, and two moved away, Erica had—and was still having—a hard time adjusting.

The inquisition stopped, anyway, when the kids raced into the yard.

They roasted the chicken outside, eating with their fingers. Her dad plunked down next to her, offering his knee as a backrest and keeping the clan regaled with fish stories and jokes. Karen would have asked if there was something on his mind, but there was no chance. Cold and darkness eventually chased them all inside, and they huddled over the game table, playing canasta and Scrabble. The mountain air caught up with them and started an infectious spiral of yawns. Julie dropped out first, then the others, one by one. With a crowd, the girls camped in one bedroom and the boys in the other.

Karen banked the fireplace fire. For a while she heard her father talking to Jon Jacob and smiled at the man-to-man murmurs. Eventually, though, the cabin fell silent. Everyone was asleep.

Except for her. A restless, edgy mood had been sneaking up on her all evening. Tugging on a wool-lined parka, she stepped outside. The night was cold, the bite sharp enough to make her cheeks flame. The mountains rose like ghosts in the distance, and spears of icy white moonlight shot through the ravine. She shivered, yet made no move to go back inside.

Hours before, her mother's prying questions hadn't bothered her. But they did now. Technically her mom had asked the same kinds of questions a zillion times since she was knee-high, but Karen was aware of the difference. It wasn't just her mom. Her dad had been unusually protective tonight. Jon Jacob had thoroughly grilled her about the "anonymous" gift of cherries in the mail. Julie was suddenly discussing men with her.

If they didn't know about Craig, they would soon. No secret kept long in her family. They were simply too close.

Karen closed her eyes and inhaled a lungful of sharp dry air. *So why are you still waiting to tell them? He loves you. You love him. You both want the same thing—to get back together. So what's holding you back?*

But she knew that answer. Her fingers closed tightly on the rough porch railing. The joy they were finding in each other was as real as her own heartbeat. They were talking... like they hadn't talked in years. And their physical intimacy... she'd never doubted they were good together, but what they brought each other in passion now obliterated anything she'd ever felt before.

She'd needed it all. Needed to explore, to experiment, to learn things about herself as a woman. Needed to know that she'd changed, that she could come to him as an equal, that she could be more than the backseat partner she'd been in the past.

None of that could have happened without private time—time to know Craig one-on-one—but their secret relationship had the same catch-22. They were still living in an ivory tower. And Karen simply had no way to evaluate if Craig would feel the same way about her when the excitement of pursuit and seduction was done. Romance had a nasty way of dying when two people brushed their teeth together in the morning.

She didn't know how to be sure.

She didn't know what to do.

Quiet as a whisper, the back door unlatched. Her mother, huddled in Walt's oversize hunting jacket, stepped outside in her slippers.

"Mom, you'll catch your death," Karen scolded.

"Hmm." Erica Hennessey inhaled the cold night air, noted the crunch of frost on the grass and decided they were both going to die of pneumonia. But she ambled next to her daughter.

"Mom, I'm *fine*. I just needed a few minutes of fresh air."

Her mother nodded. "It was always easier for you to talk with your dad than me. No criticism intended, sweetheart. I always liked it that you two were kindred spirits. But it finally occurred to me that your father guessed what I didn't. It's a man, isn't it?"

"Mom—"

"You changed your hair. Your makeup. You're in the middle of a conversation and suddenly you get this smile on your face. You lost at canasta. Usually you have to throw the game to make us win...so it's definitely a man. You love him?"

For a moment Karen couldn't answer. Her mother wasn't looking at her, but staring busily at a raccoon edging into the yard. A mom, giving her daughter "space." The way she tried to hard to give Julie "space."

Maybe they'd never been close—not like she and her dad—but in the past years, they'd both been trying. Karen said finally, "Samantha and June...they headed straight for successful careers and marriages. They never did anything to disappoint you."

"Neither did you, Karen Amelia."

Karen shook her head. "You know better. I had the grades in school, but no sure direction then. And it hurt you both when Craig and I eloped. It hurt you more when we divorced. I felt like...I always felt like...I was failing you."

"Idiot." Erica may have never fully understood her youngest, but her maternal instinct was to call a spade a spade. "You were always your father's favorite.

Surely you know that. You couldn't fail him if you dug ditches—''

"Not him, Mom. You. I thought I'd failed you."

Erica turned her head and gently studied her daughter's moonlit features. "You're out of your mind, darling. I never cared what you did as long as you were happy. Unfortunately you're like your father. Quietly, automatically taking care of other people's needs, but like a mummy about your own. You always kept your hurts in, your worries, your fears. I used to walk the floors, scared to bits you'd get taken in by some selfish man who didn't realize how vulnerable you were. And that's exactly what happened—''

"No," Karen interjected swiftly. "I want you to stop blaming him, Mom. You always liked Craig, until you thought that he hurt me. But it wasn't that way. I hurt myself. I never stood on my own two feet. I depended on him instead of myself. Any relationship I had would have floundered.''

"Maybe."

"Not *maybe*. That's the way it was."

Their eyes met in the darkness, not mother and daughter in that instant, but woman and woman. "So it *is* a man," Erica said softly.

Karen nodded.

"A man who seriously matters to you."

Karen nodded again.

"I expect," her mother said cautiously, "that you'd already have told me if you thought I would approve."

"Not in the beginning, you won't," Karen admitted. "But that's not what's holding me back."

"Good. Because I can promise you, Karen Amelia, that if he'll make you happy, I really won't care if he's a Democrat." It was a small joke, but it finally won her daughter's smile. Erica abruptly sobered. "Just be sure, honey—be very sure—that you never go into another relationship with stars in your eyes."

Ten

"Craig...I know this is going to sound a little crazy...but could you do your best to pick a fight with me?"

The towel dropped from his hand. Seconds before, he'd pelted from the shower to catch the phone. He'd hoped it would be Kara—and it was. And he'd hoped she would call, even this late on a Sunday night, to let him know how the camping weekend had gone with her parents.

But he definitely hadn't expected that opening line for a greeting. "A fight?" he echoed blankly.

"An honest fight. A real fight. I know it sounds strange, but if you think about it...we haven't disagreed about anything, haven't had a single argument. It's like we're going around with stars in our eyes."

She actually sounded serious.

"So..." Craig swiped a hand over his face and let the towel lie. No one was going to know if he walked through his own house dripping and stark naked. Carting the traveling phone, he headed directly for the kitchen cupboard that stocked the Scotch. "So..." he said tactfully, "you think it would solve something if we had a fight?"

Silence. "Okay, I can hear it in your voice. You think the idea's off-the-wall. And it probably is. I'm sorry I brought it up."

He heard the uncertain tremor in her tone and suddenly felt knee-deep in quicksand. "Hey, I never said the idea was off-the-wall." He poured a quick shot, thinking that the idea was pure bananas and that he'd give diamonds for some inkling into the irrational vagaries of the feminine mind. When he left Kara on Friday, she'd been *fine*. They'd been doing great. Damn it, what had happened to scare her?

"Craig? Are you there?"

"I'm here. I was just thinking that it might be a tad tricky to get into an argument just like that. I mean . . . it takes a mood."

"It didn't used to take a mood. We used to fight at the drop of a hat. Which is the point. Sooner or later, we *are* going to argue about something, and fighting is one of those things we used to be terrible at, and if we just tried—"

"Okay, okay." He cleared his throat. "If you wanna fight, sunshine, we'll fight. But not on the phone."

Karen never liked leaving the kids alone, but they were both asleep this late on a Sunday night, and Craig was determined to see her face-to-face. Waiting for her to arrive, he started a pot of coffee and then hastily pulled on a flannel shirt and jeans. He never had the chance to brush his hair before she rapped on his back door.

If she'd been through some trauma, it didn't show. She breezed in, all flushed cheeks and vibrant energy, and whisked past him. She peeled off her coat and shoes, revealing an oversize red shirt and snug jeans. Fightin' clothes. Barefoot, she aimed directly for his living room and rolled up her cuffs.

He didn't dare smile, but, Lord, he was tempted. Her hair was just washed, flyaway silk, and she hadn't taken the time to put on a bra. Her breasts heaved alluringly with every agitated breath. He could think of a lot of things he wanted to do with her just then. None of them including fighting.

"You want coffee?"

Not then. Right then she just wanted to pace the length of his living room with a determined scowl. Finally her finger came up and wagged at him. "You were selfish," she accused him. "So wrapped up in your work that you didn't notice anything that was happening to me."

"I know, honey."

Her face fell. She sighed heavily. "Craig, Craig, Craig. You're not getting in the spirit of this. Don't agree with me. *Defend.* Argue. Fight."

"Okay."

"Besides, you were never that selfish. Half the blame was mine. I never opened my mouth to tell you when things were going wrong, so how could you have known?" She waved a hand impatiently. "We're getting off the track. We have to find something we *know* we disagree about.''

Until that instant, Craig had been prepared to cater to her with patience and masculine tolerance. Picking a fight out of thin air was nuts. Any man would know that. God knew where this whim of hers came from. Two days with her mother? One of those tests in women's magazines that she liked to take?

Yet he felt a twist of poignant understanding when he looked, really looked, at her face. Karen was in no more mood to stage some artificial spat than he was, but this was no joke. Not to her. There was apprehension in her eyes, anxiety. Kara had never been easily assertive, but she did have a temper. Both of them had been stupid about holding hurts in; then would come an explosion out of proportion over little things. Kara had reason to remember those fights, reason to need assurance—and reassurance—that they wouldn't fall into that well pit again.

Maybe he did, too.

"Okay," Craig said. "You want to get down and dirty, we'll do it."

Finally, Karen thought, he was taking her seriously. Or so she hoped.

They went through a pot of Amarillo on the situation in the Middle East, his mother, her mother, local politics and money. The one subject—money—should have guaranteed a quarrel as sure as the sun came up in the morning. Craig was free with a dollar. She was a saver. The straw that broke the camel's back had been some stupid war about money.

Only nothing worked this time. They certainly disagreed, but Craig, damn him, listened to her point of view. Even the subject of money failed to start war. Craig admitted honestly that budgets were probably always going to be a source of friction, but, in reality, they were good for each other. Their different perspective made for a successful balance.

Karen sprang to her feet. "You're not even trying," she said irritably.

"I am. I am."

"Well, not hard enough. For cripes' sake, at this point, we could sell a self-help book on marital fights. That isn't how it was. Come on, try and remember the last time you were angry with me. *Really* angry with me."

"The MG convertible."

Finally a look of happiness in her eyes. "Oh, Lord, were you mad."

"We'd just got it. The ink on the title was hardly dry. I'd had the engine overhauled, new paint, new parts. It was the first fun thing we could afford, the first luxury that we didn't have to feel guilty about. And you wrapped it around a tree." Suddenly he was on his feet, too.

"You wanted to kill me."

"You could have *been* killed. Driving too fast on a snowy night, and all to hurry home with a stupid quart of milk."

"When the policeman drove me home, you were nice," she recalled. "Until he was gone and we were alone. You threw something at me, Reardon."

"Yeah, I did." As he recalled, it was a couch pillow. Thrown hard enough—not at her, but at a wall—to make the seams pop and feathers snow all over both of them.

"You were spitting fire."

"You bet I was. What made me madder than anything else was you thinking I cared more about the damned car than you."

"Reardon?"

"Hmm?"

"You're losing the entire spirit of this exercise. We're supposed to be fighting. I've been trying my darnedest to make you angry."

"Sunshine, it worked. I'm furious with you."

"You're unbuttoning my shirt. This is not a sign of anger. And I have to tell you something. Something serious. I've been waiting for the right time, only a 'right time' just doesn't seem to happen, and it's something I need you to know."

Once he'd thumbed open two of her shirt buttons and discovered bare skin, it was difficult to regain his attention. She was having the same problem concentrating. They'd actually done it—waded into rough waters, with no stars of romance in either of their eyes, and managed fine. No magic. Just honesty and sharing, and the song in her heart was very hard to ignore.

But Karen had been quiet before, had failed to say things that mattered. Firmly she framed his face in her hands. "I just want you to know," she said softly. "I was always proud of you, Craig. Always. Your parents blitzed you when they split up, but even when we were kids, you never let on that their life-styles bothered you. You just went your own way—always stood up for what you believed in, made your own road, danced to nobody's drummer. Even when we were going through rough times...that never changed. I was always proud of you. The boy you were, and the man you became.''

She saw him swallow, saw his jaw working hard to swallow a second time. He said, ''Damn it, Kara,'' in a voice so thick with emotion that it never reached a whisper. And then, even softer, ''Now you've *really* made me mad.''

''Yeah?'' She smiled. And then reached for him.

Three days later, Craig was in the office, finishing up a business call, when he heard voices outside the door.

''I assume that he's busy, Virginia, but I was already across town on an errand for my boss, and I only need to see him for a second—''

''It's okay. I'll buzz him.''

''It's something about the children.''

''I'm sure it is.''

''If he's in the middle of something, I could just leave this on his desk—''

Craig cut short the phone call when he recognized Karen's voice, but he missed the rest of the conversation because Virginia jammed a finger on his call buzzer. The unrelenting buzz didn't cease until he appeared in the doorway, when his assistant promptly lifted her finger and beamed him an innocent, near-beatific smile.

''Mrs. Reardon was trying to leave without seeing you.'' Virginia popped to her feet and efficiently herded Karen toward him. ''As if you couldn't spare a few minutes on something about the *children*. I'll just hold your calls for a bit. Don't either of you worry about a thing. In fact, it's been such a madhouse today that I'll just close this door to shut out some of the noise...."

Actually, Craig closed the door before his assistant could ramble on in that nauseatingly sweet tone for another five minutes. He'd never said a word to Ginny about Karen. Nothing. Nada. But her heavy-handed helpfulness was so out of character that Karen was likely to suspect—as he did—that Virginia was on to them. Later, he'd talk to her.

Right now, there was only one woman on his mind.

Once the door was closed, Karen pivoted to face him. She was wearing a winter-white blazer over a navy dress, and clutching a cumbersome yellow sack with both hands. He'd seen the dress and blazer before. But the rosy glow on her skin...that was new. The unquenchable sparkle in her eyes...that was new, too.

They'd crossed a land mine on that crazy night she'd insisted on fighting. If Craig had realized some critical test was at stake, he would have been petrified. He hadn't known, and didn't care how or why that night made such a difference. It had. All that mattered. Her smile was like the flame of a candle, lit from within, and that smile was for him. The love in her eyes was open, honest, unhidden. That love was for him, too.

Momentarily, though, she was flustered—hugging that huge yellow bag and making fast excuses for her impromptu visit to his office. "I really didn't mean to interrupt your workday. But when I realized neither of us could get away for lunch...well. This was something that couldn't wait until tomorrow."

"No?"

"No," she echoed. "One of us is thirty-seven to-day. Poor baby, you're getting to be such an old man. I just couldn't let you suffer alone—"

He severed the space between them in three strides. She seemed to expect some retribution for the insult because she lifted her face. He caught a whiff of honeysuckle and rose when he claimed a kiss.

It should have lessened by now, he thought. The hunger, the excitement, the urgency of his physical desire for her should have been appeased. But it seemed some nasty result of this new and growing love between them. He couldn't get enough. He had the terrible feeling that at the rare age of ninety, he'd still never have enough of Kara.

Her lips molded under his, shaped under his, as if she was suffering the same shameless problem. Time kindly slowed. The peripheral world kindly blurred. Whether Kara was aware—surely she was—there was no caution or wariness in her response now. She welcomed him in her arms with longing in her eyes and belonging in her touch.

Karen broke off the kiss, breathless and flushed. "Darn it, Craig, that was *not* what I came for. Now behave," she scolded, as if he were at fault for playing with matches. Wriggling away from him, she reached for the yellow bag. "First, I have to tell you a couple of things. You need to be home by six."

"Six?"

She nodded vigorously. "The kids are going to be there—which you're not supposed to know, so act surprised. And be careful. The cake tilts like the leaning tower of Pisa. Julie did the cake and Jon's planning on having dinner ready, and you need to be tactful about that, too, because the last time I tasted our son's spaghetti—''

''I'll be surprised. I'll be tactful.'' He hated birthday celebrations. Kara had always loved them. It was in her eyes, that she'd had a hand in the cake and the surprise dinner. But he caught something else in her expression, too. Regret, frustration. She couldn't, of course, be there. She was an ex-wife. Someone who had to invent excuses to his secretary to see him. Someone who had no right to share a holiday or birthday celebration with him.

She quickly smiled, though, and from the yellow bag she pulled out a square package, wrapped with shiny paper and a gigantic bow.

''Now, don't give me a hard time. I already know— the only thing you hate more than birthday celebrations is knowing what to do or say about gifts. But you'll just have to bear up. This is just a little something, anyway.''

It wasn't a ''little something,'' but a sweater that she'd knit herself, cream colored and cabled down the front. Karen was so excited she couldn't stand still. She pushed off his suit coat, helped him pull it over his head. And then her face fell. ''I made the sleeves too long.''

''No, you didn't. This is perfect.'' He cuffed the sleeves twice, quickly. ''Sunshine, it's the most beautiful sweater I ever had.''

''I made it at night. So the kids wouldn't realize it was from me, and you wouldn't have to worry about when you wore it,'' she said in a rush, making him aware how much that bothered her. But then she stepped back, cocked her head to study him with an impishly arched brow. "Is the neck too loose?"

"No. It's just right."

"The sleeves—"

"Are perfect."

She promptly lost interest in the fit of the sweater. Her gaze dawdled down the length of him, then swiveled slowly back to his eyes. "I'll be darned. You're good-looking. Not just handsome, but the sexiest man I've seen this side of the Continental Divide. Amazing, at your advanced age—"

He crooked his finger at her.

Laughing, she shook her head. "I *really* have to get back to work. I had an errand for Jim, but he'll be expecting me back and there's a mountain of work waiting at the office—"

But she didn't protest all that hard when he captured her hands and yoked them around his neck. If she was expecting a kiss, she didn't get one. He simply held her, hugging her against his heartbeat, cradling her in the nest of his arms. She fit him, like a lock and key, like a part of his heart was missing without her. He thought, *it has to be time.*

"Kara?" He nuzzled her cheek. "I love the sweater." He saw the mist of emotion in her eyes. Her mind wasn't on the sweater, nor was his. "But there's something else I would really like for my birthday."

"What?"

"I *love* you, sunshine. And I want the right to come home to you, the right to tell the world how I feel about you. I want my ring on your finger. I want to be with you, not just for quick stolen moments but for the rest of our lives. And I hope...I think...you want that as much as I do."

He was afraid she would stiffen in his arms, pull away. But she didn't. She lifted her head and openly revealed the depth of her feelings for him, in her eyes, her face. Yet she said nothing.

"Are you afraid? Of how the kids will respond?"

She shook her head. "No. They've wanted us back together all along."

"If you're worried about your mother, I'll talk to her first, Kara, or else we can do it together."

She shook her head again, this time violently. "Craig... I'm not afraid of facing anyone. I never was. It was just that there are people who love and care about us, and I didn't want their hopes built up—or their worries—until we were sure."

"I *am* sure."

She started to say something—and then jumped, startled, when she heard voices in the next office. The distraction changed her whole mood. "We can't talk about this now. No, don't look like that, please. I love you, Craig." Her tone lowered, softened to velvet. "*Really* love you. More than before. More than I ever thought was possible. I just want the chance to talk alone with you first, okay?"

Craig let her go.

A week later, he wished he hadn't. Because something happened in that week to make Kara decide that she didn't want him in her life. At all.

The kids had just left for his birthday party...where she belonged, where she wanted to be, with all of them together as a family again. Karen heard the furnace turn on, the tick of the kitchen clock. The whole house echoed with cavernously lonely sounds.

Tomorrow, she consoled herself, it would all be different.

Opening the refrigerator, she rummaged through the shelves for something to snack on. She found a wedge of cheese and a leftover bowl of tapioca pudding, but neither taste appealed. In the back, behind a hunk of lettuce, was a jar of olives. It would do.

Carting the jar, she nudged the fridge door closed with her hip, and distractedly popped one olive. Then a second.

She couldn't wait to talk with Craig. It still ached, recalling the look of hurt in his eyes when she hadn't instantly given him a "yes" that morning. To hurt him... Lord, she hadn't meant to. But there were people in his office and a job she had to rush back to. He wanted a commitment from her—and he would have it, from her heart—but she needed uninterrupted time to tell him her own way.

Roaming toward the living room, she scooped another couple olives from the jar.

From the start, she'd been afraid of losing the magic if they settled down. She'd been wrong. Nothing was the same in their relationship now. They'd learned how to communicate. They'd both strived to change, and been rewarded by a stronger, deeper love because of those real changes. And as far as the magic... Karen finally realized that magic wasn't a mystical surprise or a component of chemistry. Magic was about making time, private time, for each other. It was something that a woman could make happen...if she dived deep, and felt secure enough in the right kind of love, to experiment and explore.

In the front hall she flipped on the porch light for the kids. Tomorrow she'd tell him. She would be, wanted to be, a different kind of wife for him this time. She'd tell him at lunch. A long, private, romantic lunch. The kind of lunch she hoped to have with him until they were one hundred and ten.

Glancing out the window—the kids should be walking home from Craig's soon—she dipped her finger in the jar for another olive...and came up empty.

Absently she glanced down. It was hard to believe she'd leveled the whole jar. In fact, impossible. She'd always liked black olives, but the only time that she'd ever guzzled them like a kid with candy was when she was pregnant.

The thought struck her as humorous.

And then not so humorous.

She couldn't, she told herself, be pregnant. Neither of them had been irresponsible about birth control. She'd been prepared. So had Craig. He'd not only told her, but showed her, that he would never risk her again like when they were teenagers.

Yet Karen's feet were suddenly skimming down the hall toward the back bathroom, where a calendar hung next to the sink. She wasn't always regular and they'd been careful, but her mind spun back, remembering...Lord, remembering!...that one time. The first time. In the cabin, when neither of them had conceivably anticipated that a simple kiss would explode into a conflagration. Neither of them had been prepared then.

●

And the calendar claimed she was two weeks late.

She sank on the covered seat of the john, and was still there twenty minutes later when Jon and Julie bounded in the back door. The kids were bouncing and exuberant, talking ten for a dozen about the success of their ''surprise'' birthday for their dad. Craig had done a lion's job of raving about dinner and the cake and his presents.

Karen heard herself laughing, heard herself saying and doing all the normal things with the kids. It was a school night. Julie still had some history notes to go over before a test, Jon had trash to take out, and the crew migrated to the den for an hour of TV before bed. Finally Julie ambled upstairs. Karen told them both that she would be up in a few minutes and headed for the kitchen with her hands full of dirty glasses.

''Mom . . . you could have come.''

She turned. As desperately as she craved a moment alone, apparently it wasn't to be. Jon Jacob hovered in the doorway, his hands dug in his jeans pockets. ''Come where, honey?''

''To Dad's. A birthday isn't the same without you there, and Dad missed you.'' Jon shifted on his feet. ''It's okay, Mom. We *know*.''

''You know what, sport?'' Karen thought, Please, God, don't give me a second heart attack to deal with tonight.

''We know you're seeing Dad. Like, it took a while for Julie to figure it out, but she's just a kid yet. I guessed why you didn't want to say anything. You were worried we'd start pushing you to get back together, right? But we'd never do that again. You guys take your time.'' Jon raked a hand through his hair in a gesture Karen had seen his father do a zillion times. "If it works out, it works out. If it doesn't, it doesn't. Right?"

Karen's throat was suddenly drier than a parched cactus. "Right."

"Like everything's copacetic. You guys want to go out to dinner, stuff like that, it's okay. You don't have to worry about us. Julie started asking me some dumb questions, like if there'd be another wedding, if she'd be in it. I told her to shut up," he said reassuringly.

Jon saved her the need for a reply. He yawned hugely, claimed he wanted to catch a shower before bed and rambled upstairs. In short order, Karen was alone.

Totally alone. So alone that the walls of the kitchen seemed to close in on her. If there was oxygen in the house, her lungs couldn't seem to find it, and her stomach was rolling and pitching like a raft in an upset sea.

So, she thought, their secret was out. No major surprise. There had never been a chance that she and Craig could keep their secret forever. Only now she had another secret.

And this one changed everything.

She closed her eyes, sick with anxiety—and despair. In the past weeks, they'd relived a lot of their old history. But this was not, definitely not, the patch of their old history that she could bear putting him through again.

They were still rediscovering each other. She'd just come to understand how the weight of old mistakes had preyed on Craig. With enough private time together, Karen felt confident that the old black magic between them could be nurtured, strengthened. Craig needed to know that he was valued—not just as father and husband and responsible breadwinner—but at the vulnerable level of lover.

She couldn't do it to him again. She just couldn't. They'd been through this, exactly this, seventeen years ago. She adored the children. So did Craig. But a pregnancy completely changed the nature of a relationship, and a surprise pregnancy forced changes before a couple might be ready to cope with them. It was true then. And just as true now.

A penchant for olives and a tardy date on a calendar was hardly proof. As soon as possible, she would see a doctor. But in her heart—and, Lord, her heart was still pounding like a thudding hammer—she knew.

And there was no possible way she could keep this secret for long.

Eleven

————

"Jim, this is Craig Reardon. Is Karen there, please?"

"She sure is. Just a second." But seconds passed, and then a full minute before Karen's boss returned to the line. "Well, she *was* here. She must have slipped off to the ladies' room. I'll leave her a message to call you back."

"I'd appreciate that. Thanks."

Craig hung up the receiver. Fifteen minutes later, Virginia poked her head around the door to announce it was five and a Friday night in case he'd forgotten and she was headed home.

So was everyone else. People shuttled down the hall in a mass exodus. Even the die-hard workaholics left promptly on Friday. Within minutes the office had cleared out, and still Craig sat glued in his office chair...waiting for a phone that he already suspected wasn't going to ring.

In the four days since his birthday, he'd talked to Karen twice. On both occasions she'd called to cancel getting together at noon and then hustled off the phone with an excuse. When he tried to call her at home, she was suddenly in the bathtub. When he called at work, by the time the switchboard operator connected to her office, she was suddenly in the rest room or away from her desk. None of his calls were returned.

It was possible, of course, that she was honestly busy.

And cats swam.

Craig dragged a hand through his hair. For days his stomach had been in knots, and now dread sludged through his pulse. He couldn't continue to pretend that everything was fine, when something was obviously wrong. Disastrously wrong.

Maybe he'd pushed her too fast to get back together. Maybe she'd taken another look at his track record and decided he wasn't worth the risk. Maybe she'd looked in her heart and discovered that she simply didn't love him.

The fear of losing her weighed him down like a ten-ton rock sitting on his chest.

He told himself that even if Karen had changed her mind, it was totally unlike her to run. Kara faced things head-on—sometimes too fast and sometimes bullheadedly—but she never avoided a tough situation. If she wanted to call it off, she would have said so. She never sat on trouble. She got it over with.

So you want to believe, Reardon. But the reality is that she's avoiding you. She doesn't want to see you. Or talk to you. Or, apparently, be anywhere around you.

He waited for the telephone to ring until six, then left the office. At home he popped a frozen dinner in the microwave, then couldn't eat it. He brewed a pot of coffee, then ignored it, too. He showered, shaved, changed clothes, turned the TV on, then off, then paced. Nothing did any good. He felt as if he was unravelling at the seams. One way or another, he had to reach her.

The traveling phone paced the house with him for the next two hours. The kids invariably had something going on a Friday night, which meant it should have been an ideal chance to catch her alone. Yet there was no answer, time after time, until the line connected just after eleven.

When a sleepy-voiced man answered the phone, Craig felt his stomach drop clear through the floor. It took him a scrambling second to recognize that it was only her father.

"She's not here," Walt told him.

Craig had had enough. "Of course she's there. It's eleven o'clock at night."

"I know what time it is—" Walt's groggy tone suddenly snapped awake "—and I thought she was with you. The kids just came home from a ball game. I'm spending the night on some dang-fool excuse about checking her furnace. She told her mother it hisses in the middle of the night. I didn't say a word. I assumed you two wanted some time alone, so I pitched in. The furnace was just an excuse to stay over with the kids without looking like a baby-sitter. The kids, of course, think they're plenty old enough to..." Abruptly he cut off the lengthy explanations. "Tarnation. If *you* don't know where she is—"

Hearing the worry in her father's voice, Craig automatically reassured the older man. "It's all right. I know where she is."

"Because if she isn't with you, she's alone, and this late at night—"

"Walt, we had a mix-up about places. That's all. Nothing's wrong, nothing's happened to her. I know where she is and you know damn well I'll take care of her."

Big promises for a man whose knees were knocking. Yet from the instant her father started talking, Craig's mind had been spinning at a hundred miles an hour. Now, as soon as he hung up, he yanked on a jacket and grabbed the keys for the Cherokee. He made a stop at a drugstore, then another stop for gas where he picked up a cup of strong coffee, then headed straight for the mountains.

The night was a moonless black, the roads deserted this late. The miles blurred past, his car lights like beacons on the lonely blacktop, his accelerator flattened until he was forced to slow down for the mountain curves. His mood zippered from the soar of anticipation to the pit of anxiety.

He hadn't exactly lied to Walt. He had a good idea where Karen was.

She'd made her father believe that she was with him. That changed everything. Karen would hardly engage her father in a scheme to be away all night with a man she was about to jettison like unwanted baggage. So something was still wrong. Badly, seriously wrong. Wrong enough that she couldn't face him, wrong enough that she needed to be away from the kids, wrong enough that she wanted to disappear.

Only one problem he could imagine would upset her that badly.

And there was only one place Kara had ever sought when the world was giving her hell.

It was two in the morning when he parked behind her Cierra. There were no lights on in the cabin, but smoke ribboned out of the chimney. He unlatched the door as quietly as he could . . . and found her.

For the first time in hours, his heartbeat slowed down.

She was curled up, knees to her chin, in a sleeping bag on the couch. Hours before, she must have stacked a mountain of wood in the hearth. Now the fire had dwindled down to a heaped bed of sizzling amber coals. The firelight glowed on her skin and made her hair look like tousled gold silk.

With his gaze on the shadows of exhaustion under her eyes, he skimmed off his boots and jacket. After feeding the fire, he dropped in the oversize chair across from her. She never stirred. Craig expected that a herd of elephants wouldn't waken her, not tonight. Kara was simply beat. She'd been handling an enormous amount of stress . . . alone.

He hunched forward, watching her sleep, thinking that he'd vowed to never cause her trouble again. Thinking of all those times he'd wanted to make things right for her, and failed. Thinking that part of him was still that brash cocky boy who'd wanted, so badly, to slay all her dragons.

Thinking that he was scared, straight to the soul, that his golden girl might not give him one last chance.

Karen awakened slowly, just past dawn. Pale yellow light filtered through the windows. A huge bed of embers shimmered in the hearth and the room was toast warm. She turned on her side ... and spotted a narrow box with a drugstore label on the coffee table.

Her pulse stopped, then kicked in double time.

The box held a home pregnancy test, and just beyond it was a jeans-clad knee. Her gaze traveled from Craig's long legs to his rumpled chamois shirt to his face. He was asleep, his shoulder cramped in the chair, his cheeks stubbled with whiskers and his temples lined with exhaustion.

A lump lodged in her throat that felt as big as a football.

Craig must have sensed her studying him, because he woke with the speed of a gunshot. His dark eyes searched for, found her, in the timespan of a second.

Her heart squeezed tight. Lord, what had she done? She saw love in his gaze, so much love that she felt surrounded by it. Yet he met her eyes with an expression so strained with uncertainty and anxiety that guilt razored through her. In waiting to talk to him—in so lovingly wanting only to protect him—she had obviously badly hurt him.

"So..." he said softly, "it seems like we could be in a little trouble, sunshine. Just like old times."

She swallowed hard. "You guessed."

"Which I should have weeks ago. There was a time I knew your body better than I knew my own. The clue was obvious once I started thinking about it."

"Craig... I wouldn't have kept it from you. But next Tuesday was the soonest appointment I could get with my doctor. I didn't want to worry you unless I had to, and until then I don't know anything for sure."

"I figured you might not have had time to see the doctor yet. That's why I brought the test." He ducked his head and reached for the blue rectangular box, deliberately making his tone light and easy. "I've about got these instructions memorized. It seems we're looking for a little sucker called human chorionic gonadotropin. That's the pregnancy hormone. The whole thing's real easy, real quick. There are two windows on the handle. In the little window, you get a blue line when the test is done. Should take about three minutes. In the big window, if you get any blue at all, then we're talking about a potential miniature Reardon."

"Craig—" She heard the instructions. She wasn't against the test. But he'd stopped looking at her face and she had no idea what he was feeling.

"No talking yet. You have to do this first thing in the morning or the test isn't as accurate. So after that, we'll talk, okay?"

But he lied. The whole time she was in the bathroom—which couldn't have been ten minutes—he never stopped talking. She could hear the floorboards creaking as he paced outside the door.

"I said it was like old times, Kara. But I promise you, it wouldn't be. Nothing would be the same. Maybe we had the kids too young, but that was never really our problem. The problem was that we let our whole lives turn into a rat race until we lost sight of each other. And that's what's different. When you know what you can lose, you're smart enough to protect and guard it. God. I can't stand this. Aren't you done yet?''

"Not quite."

Another flatfooted pace. "Baby or no baby, we're going to get a full-time housekeeper. And you're going back to school. You're going to have the time to do what *you* want, Kara. I'll pitch in. The kids'll pitch in, too. You have to get out of the habit of spoiling us all rotten. You have to get a little selfish, and damn it, sunshine, if it takes my getting tough with you—"

When Karen pulled open the door, his voice petered out. Although everything he'd said had touched her, the look of him truly made her heart ache. The drawn, harsh lines on his face...they weren't about anxiety for a pregnancy. The vulnerable blaze of emotion in his eyes...it was about her, about him, about them.

There were things she needed to say. They could wait. She surged forward and wrapped her arms around him, thinking of all the times he'd been her strength, her anchor. Wanting him to know that she could be his anchor, too.

At the first feel of her arms, his voice cracked, low and sharp. He peppered her face with fierce-soft, urgent-rough kisses. "Damn it, I thought I'd lost you. Again, Kara. I couldn't lose you again—"

She hated the gravelly pain in his voice, hated having caused it. She'd sought to protect him, never to make him unsure of her. Responding instinctively, she riffled her hands through his hair and kissed him. First a soft kiss, a welcoming, and then a seeping slow kiss of comfort and reassurance.

His drumming heartbeat gradually eased. She
wasn't going to disappear. When he started believing
it, he stopped clutching her shoulders so roughly and
his touch became a caress. She wasn't trying, had
never been trying, to escape from him. When he
started believing that, her pale pink nightshirt unraveled over her head and Craig propelled her across the
threshold of the bedroom.

"I love you," she said. "I *love* you." But words
weren't enough, were never going to be enough, not
just then. She helped him peel off his clothes. That
didn't appease him. Easing her on the cushion of the
deep bed under the eaves, coming to her naked, didn't
erase the raw need in his eyes, either.

He knew where and how to touch her. He always
had. But this was the first time her lover had ever been
ruthless about tenderness. He'd been afraid, and that
desperation flavored his kisses, dominated his slow,
consuming caresses. "You're not going anywhere," he
rasped.

"No."

"Ever."

"Ever, love. I promise you." Karen swam in emotion, in the luxury of being so exquisitely cherished,
yet showered him with the feminine power of her own
brand of cherishing. She molded his flesh as he shaped
hers. She claimed kisses as possessive, as treasuring,
as his own. And when he was at his most vulnerable,
she was there for him, as he'd always been for her.

She didn't know when their lovemaking changed.
At some point what she wanted for him—what he
wanted for her—ignited naturally into passion, a pas-

sion that spiraled too hot and too compelling to control.

Just before release shattered through her whole body, she saw Craig's eyes, by early-morning sunlight. They burned, she could have sworn, straight through to her soul. With a sense of wonder, she discovered that this was nothing like the old black magic. The spice of excitement of new love paled to lovers who'd been through fire. The spell of love they wove together came from knowing each other, intimately, completely, like no one else ever had or could. This was no black magic...but white. A bond of pure white magic forged from trust, and knowledge, and the depth of love. Her heart spun with that promise through a climb toward ecstasy and then, with him, cascaded over the peak.

For a long time after that, she couldn't seem to move. Folded in Craig's arms was the only place she wanted to be. Her body still felt liquid. Her heart refused to disengage from the overwhelming feeling of connection to him. And Craig looked the image of a wasted, satisfied lover, sprawled around her in a tangle of sheets with his eyes closed and the crease of a smile still on his mouth.

But he had to be exhausted. He'd driven half the night and spent the other half dozing in a cramped chair. Karen knew he needed some honest sleep. Carefully she tried to ease away from him . . . and felt his arm scoop her right back against his chest.

"I'm not done with you."

The threat was certainly optimistic, coming from a man who could barely find the strength to open one eye, but Karen stayed where she was. Just then, she was in the mood to cater to anything he wanted.

"We have a little unfinished business."

"I know," she murmured, and abruptly sobered. "I should have told you about the pregnancy test results right away."

"That'll wait. We have something a lot more serious to discuss than that."

She looked up, confused, and discovered that he definitely wasn't as whip tired as she'd thought. Both his eyes opened and focused on her face with unrelenting intensity. "You put me through a week of hell, sunshine, and I want to know why. I thought we'd both learned a lesson not to keep secrets or bottle things in."

"We did. We have. But this was different."

"How different?"

"Because I was afraid," she said honestly.

He shook his head. "I don't care how big or small a problem is, Kara. The next time you get scared, for God's sake, get scared *with* me. Two can bite twice as many fingernails as one, and how could you forget? Handling trouble, *together,* is one of the things we do best."

She nuzzled her cheek against the palm of his hand. "But that's exactly why I couldn't tell you," she said softly.

"Honey, that doesn't make a lick of sense."

"It did to me." She searched his eyes. "Craig... you've always rescued me, always been my hero in times of trouble, always been the best man I knew when the chips were down. But for the first time since

I've known you...you didn't have to be. When we
started this relationship, I was afraid that you were
trying to recapture our old history. Only, this past
week, I took a long look at that old history. When we
were kids, we were both serious to a fault. It was *now*
we were having fun together. Not just playing at romance, but living it.''

When he tried to interrupt, she pressed a finger on
his lips. ''I *know* you, Reardon. I know about your
guilt trips and your overdeveloped sense of responsibility. If you thought I was pregnant, you'd have a ring
jammed on my finger at the speed of sound. But I
never wanted you to feel trapped or stuck. I never
wanted you to sink back into believing that you had to
'make things right for me.' I wanted you to enjoy...us. We just found each other in the best of ways,
and I was terrified of losing that. Damn it, I want you
to be happy.''

This time, when she tried to keep talking, Craig laid
a finger on her lips. ''I was chasing you in alleys and
attics—I was seducing you in cars—I was doing my
immoral damnedest to sweep you away. Before there
was any thought of a baby. And you know that.''

She whispered, ''Yes.''

''I asked you, the day in the office, to marry me.
Before there was any thought of a baby. And you
know that, too.''

She whispered, ''Yes.''

''It's possible that I go a little overboard at the idea
of protecting you. But I'm beginning to understand
that you're even worse about trying to protect me.''
Smooth as a cat burglar, he captured her arms and
lassoed them neatly around his neck. ''A baby

wouldn't trap me, honey. If there isn't one in the nest now, there probably will be by next year. You love kids, and so do I—but that's separate from *us*. I want you in my life because I love you. Because nothing's right without you. Because you're the right half of my soul. Do we have that straight now?''

She whispered, even more softly, "Yes."

"I haven't made you a promise before—but I'm making one now. Neither tornados nor babies nor earthquakes could change what I want for us. I want time with you, time for us, and I promise you we're going to make that happen. Believe me?''

"I believe you." An overwhelming sense of rightness brought tears to her eyes. Neither of them were operating under a spell of love anymore. This white magic was grounded in cement. He wanted what she wanted, needed what she needed, and both of them had learned to make that commitment their first priority. "Reardon?" she whispered.

"Hmm?"

"We're gonna make it this time."

"Yeah, we are." His voice cracked. He had to swallow. "I love you, Kara."

"And I love you."

"No more doubts?"

"Not a single one." She kissed him. A kiss of promise. "In fact, if that marriage proposal is still open ..."

"It's still open. And you could save me an imminent heart attack if you'd just say yes. Quickly."

"Yes." She said it slowly, not to torment him but because it mattered. "Yes, to us, to a lifetime, to you. A hundred times, yes. From my heart."

The last crease of worry disappeared from his forehead. She got a kiss so wicked and long that it made her toes curl. And then she got a grin, that full-of-hell boyish grin that she'd first fallen in love with. "Then for God's sake, sunshine, do you think you might be willing to tell me the results of that pregnancy test before I go out of my mind?"

She chuckled. "We got blue."

"Honest?"

"Honest."

"We *really* got blue?"

"We *really* got blue."

He let out an exuberant whoop, so full of joy that she started to laugh. Her laughter softened, though, when he lowered his head. His mouth hovered over hers, as close as a tease, and the look in his eyes made her shiver all over.

When Craig kissed her, she could taste the seal on their future. They'd loved, lost, learned. The promises they made to each other now, Karen knew they could keep.

*   *   *   *   *

SILHOUETTE® Desire™

COMING NEXT MONTH

#733 THE CASE OF THE MISSING SECRETARY—Diana Palmer
MOST WANTED
Logan Deverell disliked disruption of his orderly life. But when secretary Kit Morris decided this bear had been left in hibernation too long, suddenly calm turned to chaos!

#734 LOVE TEXAS STYLE!—Annette Broadrick
SONS OF TEXAS
Allison Alvarez didn't need any help raising her son, especially not from rugged businessman Cole Callaway—the man who had turned his back on her and her baby fifteen long years ago....

#735 DOUBLECROSS—Mary Maxwell
Secret agent Travis Cross was hunting a murderer. But while hiding out with sexy schoolteacher Alexis Wright, he caught a case of the chicken pox, and the prescription was love!

#736 HELD HOSTAGE—Jean Barrett
When timid Regan MacLeod was stranded in the snowy wilderness with accused murderer Adam Fuller, she knew survival depended on trusting the handsome, bitter man—that and body heat....

#737 UNTOUCHED BY MAN—Laura Leone
As far as scholarly Clowance Masterson was concerned, Michael O'Grady was a disreputable swindler. But the more time they spent together, the more she fell prey to his seductive charm....

#738 NAVARRONE—Helen R. Myers
September's *Man of the Month*, Navarrone Santee, had only one priority—proving his longtime enemy was a brutal killer. But his efforts were blocked by sultry Dr. Erin Hayes.

AVAILABLE NOW:

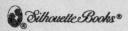

® SILHOUETTE

Desire™ 10TH

ANNIVERSARY

Anniversary

Celebrate
with
a FREE
classic
collection
of romance!

In honor of its 10th anniversary, Silhouette Desire has a gift
for you! A limited edition, hardcover anthology of three
early Silhouette Desire titles, written by three of your
favorite authors:

DIANA PALMER—*September Morning*
JENNIFER GREENE—*Body and Soul*
LASS SMALL—*To Meet Again*

This unique collection will not be available in retail stores and is
only available through this exclusive offer.

Send your name, address and zip or postal code, along with six proof-of-purchase coupons
from any Silhouette Desire published in June, July or August, plus $2.75 for postage and
handling (check or money order—please do not send cash) payable to Silhouette Books, to:

In the U.S.

Desire 10th Anniversary
Silhouette Books
3010 Walden Avenue
P.O. Box 9057
Buffalo, NY 14269-9057

In Canada

Desire 10th Anniversary
Silhouette Books
P.O. Box 609
Fort Erie, Ontario
L2A 5X3

(Please allow 4-6 weeks for delivery. Hurry! Quantities are limited. Offer expires September
30, 1992.)   SDANPOP